Ayd Instone

The Voice in the Light

and other weird tales

SUNMAKERS

Reviews of 'A Voice in the Light':

Stories to challenge and inspire the mind

"If you're looking for short stories that will not only challenge your mind whilst you read them, but also inspire you to pick up a pen and start writing your own, then this book is definitely for you. Perhaps best described as a cross between the science fiction of The Twilight Zone, mixed with the delightfully odd Britishness of Tales of the Unexpected, there should be something for everyone in this collection. Whether it's the lonely tale of a lighthouse in deep space, the disturbing case of an artificial intelligence in the frame for murder, or what really caused the Sumarian empire to crumble, each story leaves you thinking in a way that all good fiction should. At this price, for storytelling with such imagination, you really can't afford not to pick up this book."

– J Mahon

A really good humored (in every sense of the word) and intelligent read.

"I found a copy of this in the bookshelves of a library. This is really pleasant science fiction, low on nasty, pointless violence and gore, with carefully thought out and intriguing stories - it's certainly suitable for young adult readers. This is a book you can dip in and out of and it becomes obvious, the more stories you read, that the author genuinely is a scientist himself. A really good humored (in every sense of the word) and intelligent read." – S. H. Clark

A twist in the tail

"From the first story I was delighted with the clever twists and turns that took something that sounded recognisable and suddenly it was not what it seemed to be. It's a great book to read when you have a few spare moments and want to stretch your mind until it escapes from the 'box'. Ayd Instone's passion for imagination and taking the ordinary into the extraordinary is in every story."

– Lesley Morrissey

Short but powerful stories

"He presents brilliant, powerful, believable ideas in small packages. They may be short, but the concepts presented are wonderfully original and many left me reeling from being smacked around the cerebral cortex. Ayd may not write in prose (yet) but his works bring to mind Roald Dahl's short stories, the ideas of Jorge Luis Borges, and classic British horror like Alan Garner. Stories which are so rooted in reality that when they splinter away from what we know, the effect is far deeper and more believable than far fetched science fiction writings where the reader is often required to believe in and support a massive construct of science fantasy. It's my belief that anyone can learn to write, but having great ideas is a rarer gift. I believe Ayd could take his ideas to great places and personally hope he does so." – John Bloor

Unique
Totally weird! Great to read something original. Loads of succinct short stories with catchy plots and intriguing themes. Great value too." – Chris Michael

Twilight Zone fans will love this! I read it several times
"This collection is very provocative, stretching the imagination in truly untraditional ways. Often, at the end of the story, there will be one last twist that actually makes me gasp with surprised delight. Some of the tales are pure sci-fi, some are pure ghost story--and some combine the two, which is really fun. All of them will make you think. Excellent illustrations, too. They are as bold and mysterious as the tales themselves. Those zinger endings are brilliant every single time. Some of them make me cry for joy, some make me shiver with fear, and some just leave my jaw hanging. Instone has really thought about things in some mind-stretchy ways, and none of these stories feels like a parrot of some other work. The very fact that I've read the stories now three or four times each shows that I can find something new to appreciate each time through." – Mrs G.

Thought Provoking
"This collection of short stories is a gem; brimming with imaginative ideas and written so well that it is a shame when you get to the end of each, but easy to go back and read all over again. The endings are never what you think they are going to be which adds to the intrigue. Highly recommended."

– Michael Rocharde

Text ©2013 Ayd Instone

The Voice in the Light and other weird tales

Published by Sunmakers
www.sunmakers.co.uk

Version 3.0

Designed and illustrated by Ayd Instone.
Edited by Lia London, www.lialondon.net
Author photo by Haddon Davies, www.haddondavies.com

Cover image incorporates the images:
'Portrait of a mysterious young woman' by prometeus, www.123rf.com
'Walking man on a fantasy perspective space landscape' by tasosk, www.123rf.com
'Universe, planets and lots of stars' by Akirastock, www.istockphoto.com

ISBN: 978-1-908693-10-5

www.aydinstone.com

To Lia. Who made me do it.

Also by
Ayd Instone

On the Shores of Lake Onyx
and other weird tales.

Don't Tell the Dinosaurs
(The Secrets of the Future)

Ding!
How to Have a Great Idea

7 Keys to Creative Genius

Contents

A boy seeks solace from his imaginary friend from
another dimension...

At the dawn of a new millennium, three friends discover they are
witnessing the end of the world...

A robotic experiment goes disastrously wrong. But why is a
psychic detective called in?

A man's dreams become more real than waking life
as he alone learns the secret of the subterranean world beneath
The Wall...

Imagine being able to create extra time to spend as you wish.
What would you do with it?...

Could you bear the loneliness of a solitary job in deep space?

STORY AND DRAWINGS: A. INSTONE.© 1986.

Prologue

I've always preferred short stories to novels. There are two reasons I think. One is that it's so exciting to discover the one (or sometimes two) really big ideas that a short story can present that really make you stop and think. The other is that if the story's boring you can safely skip it and jump onto the next one. I hope in this collection you find more of the former.

That's my intention, to ask the question, 'What if?', to take a situation and give it just one or two big ideas, like an extra twist, at right angles to reality, to make characters twitch and a situation unfold. That, for me, is the essence of science fiction: to make just one or two changes to the universe we know about and see where those changes could lead.

Much as I love the clichéd paraphernalia of film and television science fiction; the cheeky or dangerous robots, the spaceships, the starships and the bolt cruisers, the bug-eyed monsters and the cyborgs, and as much as I expected myself to, I found I wasn't really including them in my stories.

It comes in part from the thing that non-science fiction fans hate the most; that the technobabble gets in the way of the story, or is a substitution for it. I know what they mean, and I agree. For me, in writing these stories, I had the further thought of where my imagination might be sourced. I wanted to make sure my invented worlds were as original and believable as possible and did not want to adopt or ride on the back on any pre-existing science fiction methodology. By that I mean how some authors adopt the short hand or methods of another writer. It's easy to do, but if I'm going to write about visiting other worlds, I don't want to rely on hyperdrives or warp drives, teleports or transporters, have evil empires or benevolent federations without good reason, independently arrived at. That's why most of my stories have to be drawn from something I know something about, which admittedly isn't that much. Some things are harder to avoid. If you're writing about robots, you're going to bump into Asimov who's already been down that road. If you go to Mars, you'll probably find Ray Bradbury, and if you start exploring subterranean crypts, H.P. Lovecraft will lock the door behind you.

I first started creating stories in the playground with my friend Barry. Aged eight, we became fascinated by the idea of creating a whole world-view within which to set a franchise of stories (although we'd never use or even know those words), like Flash Gordon, Star Wars and Star Trek. Barry knew about the military, so he added the workings and politics of army know-how. I was interested in spaceship and robot design and we both loved the psychological weirdness of Sapphire and Steel. Together we invented motivated villains and evil races. We concocted a reason how the Earth in the near future could engage in interstellar travel by having a 'wormhole' appear in the orbit of Jupiter. (We didn't call it a wormhole, it was a 'Time/Space Tunnel or Portal'). The playground stories became comic strips and then written down tales as we became older and the stories more sophisticated. We'd created a structure that, if published today, would seem similar to Star Trek Deep Space Nine, although our vision was created fourteen years earlier. So you won't find those tales re-told here in this collection.

Instead, I've presented here stories around the thoughts that occupy my conscious and subconscious mind: the nature of dreams, of faith, of history, time, and the nature of light. They're inspired by the kind of writers I've enjoyed, that some might call classic science fiction; Brian Aldiss, John Wyndham, Frank Herbert and Larry Niven, forgotten authors like Paul Capon and more recent deities like Douglas Adams and Philip Pullman.

Some of these stories were written over the last year, some a decade earlier, and a few over twenty-five years ago, although I'm not going to reveal which is which.

My only wish is that you enjoy reading them as much as I enjoyed writing them, and perhaps one or more of them does make you stop and ponder and think, 'that's interesting. I wonder, I wonder, I wonder...'

Ayd Instone
Oxford
March 2013

The Voice
in the Light

The Voice
in the Light

In the early days, I took her for granted. I was so young that I thought everyone had a friend like Elly. It was probably when I was around six that I realised that she was unique, or more importantly, that I was unique. I was the only one who had a secret friend, a real secret friend. To those that I told early on, I managed to backpedal later and pretend I'd made it all up and that she was just an 'imaginary friend' like a lot of kids have but grow out of. Theirs are just idle role-play or talking to their teddy. Mine was different. She was real. She came to be more real than anything, and her friendship a gift more powerful than I could have imagined.

I was teased a bit in those early days, but nothing I couldn't handle. There was nothing I was going to do to jeopardise our friendship. We needed each other, helped each other. We grew together, Elly and I. She was the only one from her world that could travel to our world. And I was the only one who could see her, or rather sense her. It was a while before I could actually see her, technically, I mean. I'll have to explain. As I said, I think I was five years old, nearly six. Dad had put the portable black and white TV in my room. Mum didn't need it while she was in hospital. The only programmes I wanted to watch were on just before the six o'clock news in those days, so I watched them on the colour TV downstairs. But having the TV in my room made me feel that I wasn't alone. I put it on when I was supposed to be asleep in bed. It had its own wire aerial, bent into a rectangle, and a dial to scroll through the bandwidth to find one of the three channels, like a radio. There was never anything in particular on; it was usually about eight o'clock at night. There was usually something like a play of some kind on BBC2. The room was filled with a soft, white light, and I watched grey images of people in costumes. It made things feel normal.

After a short while I turned it off, and the room was dark once more. Well, almost. In the centre of the screen was a single bright dot. When I looked at it, I heard a voice. When I looked away, it was gone. Looking back at the dot, the voice returned. It was a girl's voice. She was about my age, I felt. She said that talking to me was the only way she could get away from everyone, get away from all the others and their voices. She wasn't an only child like me. She said how she really wanted someone, just one special person, to be friends with. We chatted for over an hour, by which time the dot on the screen had grown faint, as had her voice. But she'd told me that she'd be back again tomorrow night if I wanted to chat again.

Mostly we talked about the things children talk about. It seemed quite natural. I knew early on that she probably wasn't from our country from how she described her days (she didn't appear to have a night), but when I had to explain other things that I thought were pretty ordinary like 'up' and 'down' (likewise she would use terms like 'through', 'split' and 'within' that confused me), I started to realise that she was really from another world. Later, of course, I'd say 'dimension' instead of world, although that might well be inaccurate.

She laughed at my concept of colours, only being able to talk about seven actual colours, whereas she talked of over two hundred (she couldn't name them all). Her world seemed to be made of colour. But what we enjoyed most was stories. She wanted to hear all the stories I could think of. I'd started off with the fairy stories I knew: Little Red Riding Hood, the Snow Queen, Rumpelstiltskin. She loved those. But I soon ran out of that kind of tale and began recounting stories I'd seen on TV. By the following year when I could read, she was hearing about the adventures of Rupert Bear, The Secret Seven, Emile and the Detectives, Stig of the Dump, Gobbolino the Witch's Cat, and then the range of Doctor Who books as I borrowed more and more books from the library to read to her at night.

Then there were her stories of the Forest of Music, the Moons of Yarn, and the Procession of Joy. Her stories were different to mine in that she was always a character in her stories. They seemed to have all happened to her, or she had been an eye witness. Perhaps that was a stylistic thing.

We must have talked, on and off, for around two years when it happened. To celebrate Mum getting better, we were going to decorate my bedroom, and I was given a new bed, a bunk bed with a desk underneath. When my Dad went to pull out the old cabinet that the portable TV was on, he hadn't realised that the TV was still plugged in. The cabinet came forward, but the TV slid off the back. There was a crash and a bang as the glass tube blew. I cried uncontrollably. He probably thought it was the shock. Mum promised to get me a new TV, although I knew they couldn't really afford one. Dad got angry. I think he was cross with himself for breaking it and muttered something about televisions shouldn't be in children's bedrooms anyway, and then this would never have happened.

We did get a new portable set for Christmas. It was a colour one. It was Boxing Day before I was able to get it into my room at night and try it. But there was no dot, no voice, no Elly.

So nearly a year passed without her. But I didn't forget. I got kicked out of both Rumbelows and Radio Rentals shops for turning all the televisions on and off, trying to find her. I didn't have many friends at that time and retreated into my books, hoping one day that I'd know her again. I started writing my own stories. I wanted to have loads of stories ready to tell Elly if she came back. I wanted to come up with something wonderful and surprising for her. It was a long wait, but it did come, and from an unsuspected place. Dad had to go into school to talk to my teachers about me. Mum was feeling poorly again.

My Dad worked at an engineering company. Occasionally he'd bring home various strange items, such as computer paper tape or machine-tooled samples. But one day, he showed me a small black plastic box, about the size of a book, with blue and white buttons on it. It was a pocket calculator. I'd seen mechanical calculators before. We used to have one, like a shop register with a spool of paper, but this fitted into my hand. I turned it on and a red segmented LED zero appeared top right under the dark opaque display. It was a scientific calculator, so I had no idea what all the buttons like sin, cos and tan did. I just typed in a few random sums.

Dad said it was a present because Mum had got sick again. So I took it up to my room to have a play after bedtime. The red LED lit up the dark room. I pressed the 8 key eight times to fill up the display with as much light as it could give. Perhaps it would be enough to read by under my covers. That's when it happened. As I looked at the display of 88888888 I heard her voice again, calling my name. It was perhaps the greatest moment of joy in my life. We picked up from where we'd left off. She told me that my star had gone out and that she'd been scanning the heavens to hear me again. From what I could make out, she used something akin to a telescope, and had tried pointing it at hundreds and hundreds of different stars when suddenly she'd heard my voice answer hers.

Elly really became a big part of my life from then on. I could carry the calculator wherever I went, and she'd always be there. I had 88888888 stored in the calculator's memory, so I only had to turn it on and press MR, and we'd be talking. The darker the room, the better though. Her voice was too faint in daylight.

She always seemed to learn more about my world than I could about hers. Not because she was evasive or undescriptive, but perhaps because I was a little bit thick and couldn't really get my head around what she was saying. She thought it was funny that we had cars to get about, or any sort of transportation that we got 'into'. I thought it meant, from how she described it, that her people flew, but she found that funny as well, as that would imply that there was a state of non-flight for flying to be flying, which there wasn't. Later I came to think that it was a bit like us taking mass for granted, and having to explain what having weight meant (I couldn't). Likewise she couldn't explain what it was like to have an attribute that, to us, would probably mean to have no concept of size. Discussions like that were all too abstract and confusing, which is why we stuck to stories about people and relationships, events and drama, which I think she understood, or came to understand. I understood most of her tales of kings and heroes, of cats and hummingbirds (or her equivalent). There were a few stories that were the same, often ones that polarised good and evil. She even had a version of the Garden of Eden, although Adam and Eve weren't thrown out of a garden, they climbed out of the water. They didn't find themselves to be 'naked' (that wasn't mentioned), but instead found they were 'heavy' (my interpretation).

Elly had a mother and father, grandparents, great grandparents, and great-great grandparents. In fact, it seemed to go on and on. They were all mentioned as if all alive and active, although I know she had a concept of death of sorts, and feared it, and she understood what I meant when it came up in my stories.

When I was ten, my parents bought me a new calculator. It had an LCD display; no light. They couldn't understand why I still carried the old clunky one around with me. I kept it even more secret.

When I was twelve and started a new school, and Mum had got better, we went on a holiday. It was the first holiday we'd been on, I think. We stayed in a small hotel by the sea and saw the switching on of Blackpool illuminations. They looked like a symphony of light. I almost felt I could hear music. When we got back home, I realised I'd lost the calculator. Mum called the hotel to see if they'd found it, but they hadn't.

I made new friends at school, did my O Levels, A Levels and even got a degree. I moved from job to job, I met someone, fell in love, fell out of love, met someone else, got married and had a son. Thomas wasn't like other boys of his age. He could never join in any games, and got angry with us and himself. At age six, he'd made no progress at school. Not able to concentrate, he couldn't write his name, or sit still, or make friends. To us, he was just Thomas, and we loved him. There were moments of clarity, and some things helped. Jane would tell me that before he'd started school, he'd pull up a little chair and sit and watch the washing machine for hours. She'd said it was the only time he'd ever shown an interest in numbers, holding a finger to the display that counted down the length of the washing cycle. But the old machine hadn't lasted long, and he'd shown no interest in the new one.

It was only as he grew older in years but not in development that we realised we couldn't really get through to him, or he to us. It was clear that the school couldn't cope with him either. There were too many reports of hitting and trouble. An educational psychologist had filed a report which led to a visit with child development people at the hospital where they talked of a spectrum of behaviour.

A neighbour noticed it first one autumn. She asked us if we knew Thomas wasn't going to sleep at night. Instead he sat at his window, staring out into the night. We took turns going up there to lift him back into bed. But one night I stopped to sit with him, hoping to see something of what he saw. It was a cloudy night. There were no stars or moon. The occasional car or bus passed (the room was at the front of the house). Was he looking at the houses opposite? The trees? I stood behind him and tried to follow his line of sight. Something was making him smile. Then he laughed. It was the first time I'd heard him laugh. The first time I could remember him smile. At first I wondered if I'd tickled him. But I hadn't. My eyes scanned the scene outside. Then I heard it. It was very faint. A voice. That voice. It was Elly's voice. He was staring at the streetlight outside the house, and Elly was telling him stories.

As I listened and stared at the street lamp, the voice changed briefly. What I'd heard at first was the voice of a six year old girl. It changed to that of a woman of my age and got briefly louder. "I'm friends with Thomas, now," Elly said.

Then the voice went dim again. Thomas laughed, and I heard her voice no more.

New Age
of Darkness

New Age
of Darkness

The planet's surface was desolate and bleak. Amongst the rocks, small plant life was sheltered from the bitter wind. The dark foreboding sky made no secret of its intentions to the rocks and the heather which braced themselves for the snow and the blizzard that would come.

But there was something else, like the calm before a storm. The landscape seemed to be holding its breath as though a great event was about to take place. An event that happened once every hundred thousand years or so, and it was long overdue.

Then, quite suddenly and without warning, nothing happened. The land breathed a sigh of relief, and the snow began to fall. Within a few hours, the planet turned its back on the sun and night fell on the moor. The only light now was an orange glow that came from one window of a large stone house. Inside were two well-dressed men. One stood by the fire, pouring brandy from an elaborate decanter into two glasses. The other, the shorter and darker of the two, sat in an extremely comfortable armchair, staring blankly out of the window.

'This will be our last drink in this century my friend,' said

Hinchcliffe, placing one of the glasses on the small oak coffee table.

'Oh, I don't know," replied Ashe. 'It's only half past ten. Surely we'll have time for another one before midnight?'

Outside the wind howled. There was still no sign of snow. Ashe pulled the burgundy velvet curtain closed. Hinchcliffe sat down opposite him.

'It was certainly a good idea of yours for us to spend the evening here instead of at some inane celebration," said Ashe, sipping the distilled beverage approvingly.

'Thank you for coming. I thought a far more appropriate way of spending the last few hours of the millennium would be for us to engage in a discussion, as you know my favourite pastime.'

'And mine,' added Ashe.

'And what better topic than the past one thousand years?'

'An awful lot to talk about.'

If Hinchcliffe's windows had not been double glazed, he would have heard the distant sound of horse hoofs on the frozen moor, getting closer and closer to the house.

'We've seen the introduction of electricity to every home, the proliferation of the automobile,' said Ashe.

'Don't forget medicine. Doctors can make life-saving decisions based on known physiology, cure most diseases, and operate on every organ in the body.'

'Genetics, of course; the discovery of our own genetic coding helix.'

The two men took it in turns to spout great advancement after great advancement.

Outside, the visitor harnessed his horse inside a stable and crossed the courtyard to the door. He opened it and slipped inside. Inside the warm room, the seemingly endless tirade of discoveries continued.

'The harnessing of atomic energy has brought...' Hinchcliffe was stopped in his tracks as a man burst through the lounge door into the room where Ashe and Hinchcliffe were sitting. Both men jumped to their feet. The stranger spoke.

'I hope in your list you've included nuclear weapons, automatic machine guns, global pollution and the destruction of the ozone layers,' said the stranger.

'Oh, it's you, Baker,"' said Hinchcliffe. 'You gave us such a fright.'

'Baker, what are you doing here? I thought you were in the city?' Ashe said.

'There is no 'city' anymore. There is no 'anything' anymore,' said Baker, still out of breath.

'What do you mean?' said Hinchcliffe.

'Sit yourself down and have a drink,' said Ashe, offering Baker a seat.

'I hope that you have included in your cosy discussion,' Baker continued, ignoring Ashe's offer of a chair, 'the fact that this century has seen destruction and cruelty on an unprecedented scale…'

'Now just a minute,' interrupted Ashe, always eager to prove someone wrong. 'You seem to be exaggerating just a little. If you want 'unprecedented scale', what about the likes of the army of Nimrod. What about Baal and Babylon?'

'Fleabitings!' snapped Baker. 'Clever men who managed to rally armies. If they were here today, they would have felt so inadequate facing the many simple ways we destroy from a distance.'

Hinchcliffe sighed. He wasn't really listening to Baker's actual words, only the sentiments, which he had encountered many times before and which always ended up with some form of confrontation. Usually it would be one that Hinchcliffe would eventually lose. Hinchcliffe sighed again at the thought of a perfectly good evening being spoiled.

'But it doesn't really matter now,' Baker hadn't stopped since he entered so unceremoniously. 'Nature has fought back. The gods have cursed us well this time. Gentlemen, the world, as we know it, has ended.'

'What?' said Hinchcliffe in mocking disbelief.

'As predictable as ever, Baker,' said Ashe. 'Always so melodramatic.'

Eventually Baker did sit down and reached for the glass Hinchcliffe had poured him. After gulping the contents down, he continued.

'At four o'clock today,' Baker began, 'the magnetic poles of the Earth flipped.'

'Really?' said Ashe, mockingly.

'It's possible, I agree,' said Hinchcliffe.

'Well, we can test it with a compass,' added Ashe.

'Yes, that window faces west,' said Hinchcliffe, going over to the mantelpiece to fetch the instrument.

'I don't think you'll find that possible,' said Baker. Hinchcliffe brought the compass over to the coffee table. He opened the brass case. Inside, the protective glass was stained with a reddish brown mottling.

'What's happened?' asked Ashe.

'I'll tell you, shall I?' responded Baker. 'This is a fairly modern house isn't it? I don't expect you have very much iron in it, fortunately.'

'Why? What do you mean?' asked Hinchcliffe.

'All iron on the planet has been oxidised.'

'What?' laughed Ashe. 'How?'

'My only guess,' continued Baker, 'is that, as the magnetic pole flipped, so too did the poles of all electrons in ferromagnetic compounds. Maybe it has affected only the iron atom, or perhaps other transition elements.'

'Yes, yes, but what does that mean?' said Ashe, a little anxious.

'Again, this is only my theory. I think that, when the pole

flipped, the electrons in iron did, too—momentarily—and it was in this split second that all iron's chemical bonds were broken. With iron being quite reactive, especially in a moist atmosphere, all the atomised iron would have instantly bonded with whatever convenient molecules were around, most probably oxygen.'

'So you're telling us that all the iron in the world, whether it was in an alloy like steel, or some other compound, has turned to rust?' said Ashe.

'It would appear so,' said Baker. 'I was just leaving the city when it happened. I looked up to see an aeroplane. It was very high up, but even from that altitude I could hear that it was having trouble with its engines. As it got closer, I knew that they had stopped. A jet aircraft is not designed for gliding, and sure enough, the heavier rear of the plane overtook the front as it hurtled down to earth. I presumed, at the time, that there must have been an explosion, but I heard none. The aircraft panels simply dropped away, leaving a plume of orange smoke as the disintegrating mass and the passengers fell to the ground to certain death. I felt sick. I knew there was nothing I could do. The crash had happened a few miles north of my position.

'But the worst was yet to come. Fortunately, I was not in the centre of town, and managed to get clear in time.'

'Get clear of what?' asked Ashe.

'Some buildings were falling down,' Baker went on. 'But the main horror came from the automobiles. The iron in them had atomised, then reacted instantly with the air to form thick clouds of tiny particles which hung in the air, choking everyone, before settling on the ground as a dusty red powder. I managed to find a horse in a field and made my way up to the moors as quickly as I could. I imagine millions will have died by now, and for those that have survived like us, it will be very difficult.'

Hinchcliffe and Ashe looked at him. They had been open-minded at first, but the story seemed much too far fetched now.

'You don't believe me?' said Baker, beginning to lose patience.

'What in this house have you got made from iron? You tell me. Go and find something.'

The two men remained seated. 'Go on. You find something.'

Hinchcliffe stood up. Baker was right. There was very little iron or steel in the house. The gas mantels that lit the room were made of brass, as was the grate and the fireplace surround. Hinchcliffe walked across the hall into the kitchen. He went straight for the cutlery drawer. He pulled. The drawer was stuck. Another heave loosened it. A great cloud of orange-red dust plumed out. Hinchcliffe coughed and spluttered. Wafting the cloud out of his face, he looked into the drawer to see it lined with more of the very fine orange powder. Not wanting to disturb more of it, he returned to the drawing room deeply unsettled, convinced now that Baker was telling the truth.

'There's one thing that bothers me,' Hinchcliffe said as he returned to his chair. The haemoglobin in blood contains iron. That doesn't seem to be affected. We would have noticed.'

'I don't know the answer to that, I'm afraid,' replied Baker.
'The phenomenon may just be restricted to bonds that iron forms in metallic compounds. In haemoglobin, it's already oxidised. It's possible that the bonds with oxygen aren't affected so strongly by magnetic fields. It's also possible that not all metallic iron is affected. If it the bonds broken by the magnetic flip could re-bond before the atomised iron gets a chance to react with anything else, it may well survive in a metallic state. Perhaps large objects, objects buried in the ground, or ones already protected by a shell of rust, may have survived intact. We can only guess at the processes involved here. What we do know is that the air is thick with ferric oxide powder, and the reservoirs, rivers and oceans will be polluted with iron. The only thing we can be sure of is that this is the end of our civilisation.'

'Oh come on, humanity will survive. We'll grow and adapt,' said Hinchcliffe.

'Of course. We've got our books, even if people do forget; we will be able to learn from our mistakes.'

'Let me tell you this. Virtually nothing is taken from one civilisation to another. We will have to start again, yes, but we will never be able to take anything from the past. Each human civilisation always assumes that it is the greatest, and that any previous one was primitive and useless by comparison. Even when evidence is found that a previous age had developed technology, that piece of evidence is overruled by the prevailing pomposity. Let me tell you this. In the future, if we do survive, no-one will know that we ever had computers or transport. If a future civilisation re-discovers iron they will have to re-learn how to extract it from its new ores. Even the knowledge of how to do that will be gone. All our knowledge has been stored on media that has now been destroyed. The older media that remain, such as films and books, will deteriorate almost completely in the centuries to come. Our civilisation's tenure on earth has been intense, but brief.'

'If what you're saying is true, with no memory carried over to the next civilisation, then we could make the same mistakes again. If our knowledge and technology advance to a similar height, we could face destruction all over again.'

'How many times has it happened already?'

\Can this really be the end of the mighty Sumerian Empire?' said Hinchcliffe. 'And all we bequeath to the future is a few crumbing stone ruins? Will the future never know the heights we reached?'

Outside the sun began to rise.

'There we have it gentlemen,' said Baker. 'The sun is all we'll have from now on to tell us what time it is. Welcome to the new age my friends, an age of darkness for all humanity.'

Project
Terminated

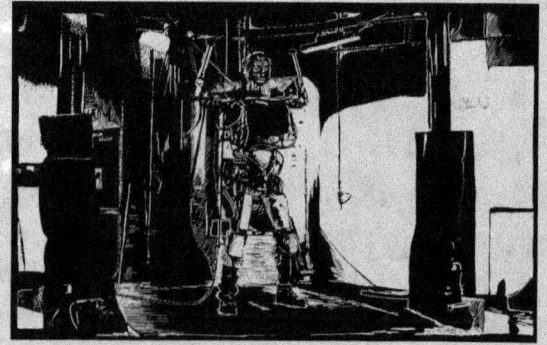

Project
Terminated

He sat in a chair, in the dark. The lab was lit only by the tiny red and green standby lights of the various electronic devices that, invisible in the darkness, lined the shelves and benches of the room. The only noise was of the air conditioning, barely audible during the day, but in the deathly silence of the early hours of the morning, the entire building seemed somehow alive.

The figure that sat in the chair was not alive. He sat slumped, with his head on one side, staring blankly ahead, his hands resting on the arms of the chair.

Paul, Ben and Greg had been drinking until the bar closed. A simple trick with a credit card had got them into the engineering block, and they slipped in as quietly as they could, but the noise of rubber on the polished floor echoed disgracefully down the dark corridor.

'Will you be quiet?' said Greg, the leader of the three to Ben, the troublemaker.

'It's the shoes, man,' said Ben. Paul, the eager-to-please fool, stifled the inane giggle that he always had.

'Where is it anyway?' said Ben.

'I was told it's next to the small electronics lab,' said Greg. 'Yeah, here.'

They all jostled to peer through the narrow windows. They saw nothing except their own stupid reflections. Ben pushed on the door.

'Aw, it's locked. What now?'

Paul had slipped back down the corridor to the door they had just passed. It opened and he slipped inside. The others followed.

The electronics lab was small, and quite well-lit due to the moonlight streaming in through the large blank windows. An adjoining door was plainly visible to the room next door. This door was locked, too.

'Try this,' whispered Paul. Greg took the key.

'Where did you get that?' Ben said.

'Never mind that now,' said Greg, sliding the key into the lock.

There was a click and the door opened. 'We're in!'

They all tiptoed into the dark, windowless room. The door swung back to close softly behind them. The room was lit only by the tiny red and green standby lights of the various electronic devices. As their eyes grew accustomed to the gloom, they could all make out the unmistakable shape of the figure slumped in the chair. An indescribable chill crawled up Greg's back. There was something not quite right about the figure and their rendezvous with it in the darkness.

Ben spoke, at normal conversation volume, shattering the bizarre silence. 'Shall I put the light on?'

'No, you idiot,' hissed Greg. 'Security will see it from the other room. If we're caught in here…'

Ben had walked over to the figure and examined its pale hands and blank expression.

'It looks quite real in the dark, don't it?' he said. 'How do we switch it on?'

'Yeah,' said Paul. 'Go on, let's see it work.'

'Don't be so stupid,' said Greg. 'I said we'd come and see it for ourselves, and there it is. We don't what to go messing with it. Do you know how much it costs?'

'Well, they've been keeping it secret. If they'd let us have a look before, we wouldn't be curious now,' Ben said. 'Come on Paul, let's find the switch.'

'There's no switches on it,' said Paul after briefly frisking the cadaver-like figure. One of the arms flopped down to hang over the side of the chair.

'It cost about two million pounds,' said Greg.

'Yeah, the two million dollar man,' sniggered Paul. 'What about this?' He'd found what appeared to be a suitable candidate for power to the chair.

'Hang on,' said Greg. But the switch had been flicked. There was a buzz and clonking sound, and the figure jolted up in the chair, then flopped down again.

'You idiots!' said Greg. 'That was like the things they use to resuscitate heart attacks. It's a fluke one of us wasn't touching the body, or we'd have been killed.'

'All right,' said Ben. 'Let's all stand clear this time. Pull the switch again, Paul.' Paul did as he was told. The figure jolted upright again and slumped back into the chair as before.

'Again!' said Ben. The figure jolted once more, but this time it did not slump pathetically back into the chair. It sat there, upright, staring blankly ahead in the near darkness.

'I don't believe it. It worked,' said Greg.

'What now?' asked Paul.

'I don't like it. It's weird,' said Ben nervously. 'It looks too… human.'

'That is the point of it,' said Greg.

'Well, is it going to do something?' said Ben. 'Come on.' He addressed the figure. 'Do something.'

'What,' replied the figure in a flat monotone voice, 'would you like me to do?'

The voice was odd. It was synthesised by an artificial voice box, and all the nuances of that voice box could be heard. It sounded somehow natural. The voice suited the shadowy figure. It had made those sounds. It had chosen what words to use in response to a question. It was waiting for a reply.

'Er, stand up,' said Ben. The figure stood up. That was all it did.

'What's your name?' asked Greg.

The figure continued to stare blankly ahead for a moment, then swiftly turned its head to face Greg. It spoke again. 'I have no memory of any name assigned to me.'

'What are you for?' asked Paul.

The head swung round to face him. 'Please rephrase your enquiry.'

'Well, what is your purpose?' asked Greg.

'To function.'

'Why?' asked Greg.

'If I cease to function, I cease to be. If I cease to be, I cannot function.'

'Paul, turn it off,' said Ben. The figure turned to look at him. The eyes did not seem so blank now. Ben backed away. There was something more behind those eyes. Anger? Hatred? Fear? Paul remained where he was, with his hand on the door handle.

'Paul, I said, turn it off,' said Ben, raising his voice.

'I advise you to do nothing,' said the cadaver calmly.

'Zap that switch when I say,' said Paul. He surged forward to shove the figure backwards, onto the chair. But the instant he touched the robot, there was a flash, a burning smell, and Paul lay still on the floor. The other two ran.

'You mean to tell me someone's been killed?' Harry Price pushed his chair back and jumped to his feet.

'Calm down, Harry. Look, sit down.' Vice-Chancellor Booth tried nervously to keep his composure. Price sat down again. Booth continued, almost in a whisper, 'It's a very delicate situation. The future of the university's funding is at stake...'

'Never mind that. Have the boy's family been informed?' Price reached for the cigarettes that weren't in his inside jacket pocket– he'd given up a year ago.

'Harry. You owe me one, remember?'

Harry did remember. It was Booth who'd helped him get started as a private detective in the first place. With his knowledge of human consciousness and psychology, he could have been a professor himself, but he'd turned away from academia a long time ago, preferring to use his knowledge, rather than just talk about it. His first assignment had been right here at the university four years ago. Now he was back again with another death. All right, he thought, I'll listen to the facts, at least.

Booth continued. 'All I ask is that you look into the situation today. Have a feel around. Use your expertise. See what you think. Then we'll talk to the boy's parents tomorrow. After I've spoken to the police.'

'We'll talk to the police right now,' said a new voice from behind Price, 'because you know as well as I do that it was no accident. The student was murdered.' Booth looked angrily at the newcomer.

'Harry Price, meet Dr Warlock, head of artificial psychic intelligence.'

The two shook hands, uncertain of each other.

'You'll remember Mr Price helped us sort out the unfortunate death of your predecessor,' said Booth.

Poor Professor Hutchins, thought Price. A brilliant scientist who'd paved the way for artificial intelligence to become the science of psychic consciousness which made the artificial brain a reality. It was a career cut short when he'd driven his car off the road. The circumstances had appeared at first suspicious, which is why Price had been involved. There had been no evidence that the incident had been anything other than a tragic accident. News of Warlock's subsequent appointment came as a surprise to Price. At the time, he'd known that the post had remained empty for over two years. That had been the point: no-one benefited from Hutchins' death.

'Nice to meet you at last, Mr Price. A shame about the circumstances. A shame, too, that your services won't be needed. This is, of course, clearly a case for the police, and I think we are long overdue in informing them of what happened here.'

Price put his hands in the air. 'Will someone please tell me what exactly has happened here?'

'Like I said,' Booth spoke quickly, 'Paul Chattersly broke into the Robotics Lab last night and somehow electrocuted himself.'

'Except we know he didn't,' said Warlock calmly. 'He was attacked by our experimental robot. There was a struggle, and the robot killed him.'

'You both seem to have a difference in opinion,' Price said.

'That's why I need you,' said Booth. 'Dr Warlock, all I'm saying is that we let Mr Price do a quick investigation first. It may have been an unfortunate accident. Then, by all means, we'll contact the police.'

Price looked around the unimpressive lab, pretending he was taking it all in. In reality, he kept one eye on Warlock and Booth who stood quietly by the door. Shelves and benches were covered in electronic equipment, all with their cases open with wires connecting to other obscure boxes and computer chasses. The only thing that made the lab different from any other electronics lab in the world was the large metal chair against one wall. In the chair was a figure, slumped, with its head on one side, staring blankly ahead, its hands resting on the arms of the chair. Price ignored the figure for a moment and walked over to study the windows. They were large, triple-glazed and locked. He looked down to the quadrangle, five floors below. Turning around, he noticed a door in the far wall.

Warlock anticipated his question. 'It leads to the adjoining lab.'

'Were both doors locked last night?' he asked.

Warlock answered. 'I believe so. Yes.'

'And who has keys?'

'Normally it would be the caretaker, the bursar and myself but, due to the nature of this particular project, the caretaker has no key. The bursar has two sets.'

Price returned to the inert form that sat in the chair. 'Tell me about the robot,' he said.

'It's the product of three years and four billion dollars' worth of sponsorship. A unique achievement to construct a humanoid robot equipped with an artificial intelligence allowing it to think and reason.'

'Can you turn it on?' said Price.

'I'm afraid that's not possible at the moment. Its brain has been removed.' Warlock indicated a dark green glass aquarium. The liquid in it looked like some kind of green jelly. Perhaps there was something floating in there. Price couldn't tell.

'Putting aside the issue of how he got in the lab, why would Chattersly come at all?' he said.

'Undergraduate prank? Drunken dare? We'll probably never know. A simple case of misadventure,' said Warlock.

'You said it cost millions. Would Chattersly know that? There must be plenty of institutions and companies willing to pay handsomely for the machine,' said Price.

'True,' said Warlock. 'The problem, however, is this: how could one student expect to get a two-hundred-and-twenty pound body out of here on his own and without being noticed?'

'Couldn't he just turn the robot on and tell it to walk out?' asked Price.

'Chattersly was not even a robotics student, let alone having particular knowledge of this experiment. The robot would not have taken orders from him, nor would even have listened to him. It would only take orders from Dr Brown and myself. That is why, if the student managed to switch the machine on, it would not have followed his orders. If he had tried to interfere with the robot in any way, anything could have happened, and it sadly looks like it did. Not only do we have a tragic death, but also the end of the project. I doubt any more sponsorship funds will be forthcoming now, even if the police allow us to continue.'

'But that means the end of your career, too, Dr Warlock,' said Price.

'Better this way than being caught trying to cover up the evidence to make it look like an accident as Dr Booth seems to be hinting at,' said Warlock.

Later, the police arrived. Price stayed until they had left. The boy's body was taken away for an autopsy, but that would only reveal the obvious. He had been electrocuted, maybe that part of it was chance, but the strangulation marks on his neck were unavoidable. The autopsy would reveal by which method Chattersly had actually died. It would be clear-cut then. Booth had wanted to somehow dodge that fact that the robot had anything to do with the student's death. Warlock insisted on it, even though that would close his department. Why was he too keen? Something he'd missed. Firstly, how did Chattersly get into the lab in the first place? Secondly, if Warlock was so intent on keeping everything above board and free from suspicion, why had he removed the robot's brain? There was something else. Something Warlock had said. Dr Booth introduced him to a few of Chattersly's associates. Price asked them a few questions before returning to Booth's office.

'So what happens to Dr Warlock now, with the robot project postponed indefinitely?'

'He's in big trouble. His knowledge will always be valuable, but there's no other big project like this that currently would need him,' said Booth.

'You were keen to clear any blame from the robot, if possible. For Warlock's sake, or your own?' said Price.

'Well both are understandable, aren't they? Obviously, I'll put the university first. But I wasn't trying to railroad the truth though. That's why I wanted you here, although it doesn't seem to have helped us in any way.'

Price continued, 'Warlock corrected you on another point. He was adamant that the student wasn't intent on stealing the robot. Now why was that? It seems perfectly reasonable to me. It shouldn't bother him either way, should it? I asked a few of the dead boy's associates what he was like. It seems Chattersly was not prone to foolishness or drunkenness. They said nothing that could rule out him being open to bribery, however. How come it was so easy for the boys to get into the room?'

'Dr Warlock said it was a simple case of misadventure, meaning that he didn't believe that a conspiracy was involved,' said Booth.

'That's it!' said Price suddenly.

'What is?' Booth said, puzzled.

'Warlock was keen to stress two things: that the robot was responsible for the death, and that there was no conspiracy. No conspiracy means no further investigation. No investigation into how Chattersly got that key. Simply close down the research project. Now who would gain from the project being terminated?'

'Only our competitors, I suppose. But there's no race to build the first humanoid robot. We're so far ahead. There would be an advantage to stealing it, but that would be discovered. No, no-one would want the project terminated,' said Booth.

'Except, of course, that's exactly what Warlock wants. He was surprisingly keen to see the end of it, and therefore his career today. He wanted to have the project ended. Not once did he attempt to defend any part of it.'

'But why?' said Booth.

It was getting late. The office's automated lights had come on some time ago. Outside it was now quite dark.

'I want to have another look at that robot,' said Price.

'But Dr Warlock has left the campus.'

'I suggest you try to get him back. In the meantime, the bursar has two sets of keys. Oh, and see if you can get hold of--what's his name?--Warlock's assistant.'

'Dr Brown,' said Booth, picking up the telephone.

They met in the corridor outside the lab; Price, Dr Brown, Booth and the bursar. Booth had told them that Warlock was on his way over. Price put the key in the lock. It wouldn't turn.

'Those were definitely the keys Dr Warlock gave me. The caretaker's set,' said the bursar worriedly.

'Let's try the other set,' said Price. The key opened the door.

The figure sat in the chair in the dark, exactly as before. Dr Brown entered first and flicked a bank of switches. Dozens of strip lights clunked and cracked into light.

'I think it would be better if Dr Warlock were here,' said Brown, nervously.

'Why?' said Price.

'Well, I just think he ought to know that you're here.'

'Why did Dr Warlock remove the robot's brain this morning?'

'Are you referring to the Autonomous Artificial Psychic unit?' said Brown

'I mean the robot's brain. The bit that makes it think,' said Price frustrated. He pointed to the green tank. 'What's in there?'

'That's the AA-Psi unit. No, he didn't remove it this morning. I removed it last night.'

'You did? Why?' said Booth.

'Dr Warlock asked me too. He said it was malfunctioning, was unstable, even dangerous.' Brown looked even more nervous than before. 'Look, I really think we should wait until Dr Warlock gets here.'

'Are you telling me that, when the death occurred, that brain unit thing wasn't in the robot's head?' said Price.

'That's right,' answered Brown. 'The Autonomous Artificial Psychic unit is only part of the robot's brain. It's the part that allows it free thought and a sense of identity--its sentience, if you like. A more traditional computer brain handles the lower functions like walking and talking.'

'And that part is still in there?' said Price.

'Yes,' said Dr Brown.

'In that case, turn the robot on,' Price said.

Brown hesitated. He looked over for approval from Booth who nodded solemnly. Brown flicked some switches and typed something on a keyboard. Price wondered to himself how a student who knew nothing of the project could have started up the robot by himself. It had to have been already on. There was a buzz and clonking sound as Brown pulled a lever. The figure jolted up in the chair, then flopped down again. Brown reset the lever and tried again. The figure jolted once more, but this time remained, upright, staring blankly ahead.

'Is this the state you leave the robot in at night?' asked Price.

'No, only if someone's here with it,' Brown replied.

The door opened and Warlock strode in. 'What's going on here?' He looked accusingly at Booth. 'You told me you would wait till I got here!' Looking over at Brown, he barked, 'What have you done?'

'Only activated it, Doctor.' replied Brown, pleased that his superior had returned, enabling him take more of a back seat.

'Not with the AA-Psi unit?' said Warlock.

'No. Would you like me to…?'

'No,' said Warlock discreetly. Then, turning to Price he asked, 'Have you seen all you want to see?'

'Almost,' said Price. He turned to the robot. 'Robot, tell me what happened last night.'

The robot said nothing.

'You won't learn anything that way, I'm afraid,' said Warlock.

'The robot's memory is stored in the AA-Psi unit and will have decayed by now, having been removed from a power source.'

'Very convenient,' said Booth under his breath. Brown walked over to the tank and looked inside. Price continued to address the robot.

'Robot, stand up.'

The robot stood up. Price pointed to Warlock. 'Put your hands around this man's neck.'

The robot advanced towards Warlock, who backed away to the closed door behind him.

'What are you doing?' he shouted. But the robot was quick. Its hands held Warlock's neck in a tight grip.

'It seems to obey my instructions after all,' said Price. 'Now Dr Warlock, what do you think would happen if I instructed the robot to tighten its grip?'

'It'll kill me!' said Warlock with difficulty. The robot's grip was not painful, but it constricted his windpipe. 'Robot, release me!

Release me!' he attempted to say, but not clearly enough for the robot to follow. Nobody moved.

'It wouldn't just kill you, Dr Warlock. It's strong enough to snap your head off. And that's exactly what would have happened if the robot had strangled the boy.'

'Did you tell Paul Chattersly to steal the robot to sell to some outside business?'

Warlock nodded reluctantly.

Price continued. 'You, of course, had the second set of keys to give to the student so he could get in. You were waiting here with the robot when he arrived. But your plan wasn't for the robot to be stolen, was it? You wanted it dismantled, destroyed. In such a way so that it could never be fully activated again. You ordered the robot to kill the student, didn't you? A murderous robot would put an end to this whole project. You had to end the experiment in disgrace – at any price.'

'I think you should release him now,' said Booth.

Price ordered the robot to return to its chair. It did so smoothly and unemotionally. Warlock coughed and rubbed his neck.

'You wired up the robot so that it was live, so that when it touched the boy, he'd be electrocuted,' said Price. 'But the resulting discharge just stunned Chattersly, didn't it? You came in and finished the job with your own hands--human hands--applying just enough pressure. You wanted to make it look like a tragic accident. Now where have I heard that before? Let's think back to the death of

Professor Hutchins five years ago. You were the one, although we didn't know at the time, who would come to benefit from his death. You took over his post, albeit it much later. You knew you were the only man capable of taking over and knew that your application would be successful and would be free of suspicion if you waited just that little while.' Price turned. 'Dr Brown, would you be kind enough to re-install the API unit into the robot's brain?'

'I'm afraid that won't be possible,' said Brown. 'The unit had been destroyed. I noticed it when we first came in. It will never work again. We'd need to grow a whole new one from scratch, and that would take years.'

'Will someone please explain why Dr Warlock would want to go to all this trouble in the first place?' asked the bursar.

Price pointed at Warlock accusingly. 'You killed Professor Hutchins so you could take his position on this project. That's how it all began. But as you worked on the project you, and only you, realised what it meant. This new auto-whatever artificial psychic brain acted as a sponge for the newly measurable, so-called 'psychic' brain activity. It worked by feeding off this psychic energy. You feared that the university somehow contained psychic energy because of the murder of Hutchins. When this unit became operational, you discovered that Hutchins's wandering spirit had taken refuge in the robot's brain. An AA-Psi unit attached to a humanoid body is the perfect vessel for a wandering spirit to possess. No spirit would ever want to possess a washing machine, or even a computer; it's just not versatile enough. A humanoid robot would allow a troubled spirit to have its revenge.'

'You mean the robot became Hutchins?' said Booth in disbelief.

'That's what Dr Warlock believed. To all intents and purposes, Hutchins came alive again and had his chance to get justice for his own murder. Warlock knew the robot was going to kill him. And only him. That's why Warlock knew he wouldn't be able to get the robot to kill the boy, so he wired up the high tension cable to do the job.'

On cue, three policemen appeared in the doorway and hand-cuffed Warlock in silence.

'What you couldn't have known,' said Booth to Warlock as he was being taken away, 'was that Harry Price is no ordinary detective. You may have been the leading theoretical psychic consciousness researcher, but Harry is the leading expert in human consciousness, and in so-called spirit possession. I suppose we could call him a psychic detective.

'If it was true, it must have been hard for Hutchins. He would have effectively died twice,' sighed Booth. 'Let's hope both he and Chattersly are at peace now.'

'I believe it was Warlock's guilt that created the belief in the possibility of spirit possession,' said Price. 'There's nothing in psychic consciousness research that I've seen that even suggests such a thing apart from the rather unfortunate name. But Warlock's fear that he'd eventually be caught created and fed a superstition. Remember this was also the first fully conscious humanoid, realistic looking robot ever made. If it had just been a voice coming from a computer, like previous AI experiments, it wouldn't have been enough. The fact that the robot looked like a walking dead man made it all the more real. It looked like a man, spoke like a man, and yet lacked the subtlety of body language that all real humans give off subconsciously, and that only added to his delusion. It became so real to him that he'd kill to free himself from it.'

As he left, Price thought to himself about what Booth had called him. 'The Psychic detective'. The scientist in him wanted to sneer. But the more he thought about it, the more it made him smile. I'll get some business cards made up, he thought to himself, and see what happens.

The Wall

The Wall

It was neither warm nor cool. The air was still. He stood on the grass in the garden with something urgent to do. Something was willing him on, perhaps against a better judgment that had left him a long time ago now. In the garden, it was day, but the sky was black. There was no sun. Perhaps there were no stars. He didn't know. He didn't look up. There was something at the bottom of the garden, waiting. Waiting underground, something menacing, drawing him towards it. The house had stood since the early 1920s, but the wall had predated that by a long, long time. It was made of the wrong stone. He knew it wasn't over that he needed to go, but under. In his hand was a spade. It took some digging. The earth was dry and dusty, easy to shift, but it kept sliding back into the hole he had just made. He worked frantically, throwing spadefuls of the brown dusty soil behind him to clear a way down. The pale grey, rough-hewn, dry stone of the wall continued down at least a foot or more before his spade slid under. There was a gap. He sat down to feel under with his hand and then, feeling tired, lay back on the ground, to relax, just for a moment.

The sun shone down through the open window. It was morning. He got up from his bed and went outside. There was still dew on the grass, and the air held the damp of late spring. There was the wall. The grass of the lawn died out as it reached the wall, shaded as it was from the leylandii and apple trees that sucked the moisture from the soil and threw a permanent shadow over the wall. But the wall was only three feet high. A wooden fence behind it was taller and hid the modern red brick of the municipal swimming pool that stood beyond it. There was no hole and no spade. The ground was untouched.

The rest of the day passed unremarkably. He managed to avoid talking at any great length with any soul, as if to save all thought processes for later on when he knew he'd need them. He re-read parts of his journal and sent off an email to Professor Jones, an archeologist at Oxford University, listing some of the most pertinent points.

It was still light when he went to bed. He'd avoided caffeine and other stimulants. He'd taken a mug of hot milk and honey. He lay there. Sleep didn't come. He saw the blue sky turn grey, then dark green, then black. Sleep didn't come. Giving up, he went downstairs and out through the back door, into the starless oppressive darkness of neither night nor day, just as before, and walked down the long narrow garden to the wall. The wall was as it had been, ten feet high of ancient, dry, grey stone. In his hand was the spade. At his feet was his ditch. He started to dig again, down over two feet deep now. The gap was big enough to get his arm through. A bit more digging and he'd be able to scramble under the wall. After a further twenty minutes of relentless but sweat-free digging, the channel was large enough to crouch down and attempt to squeeze under the gap. He got into the hole and tried to make himself as compact as he could. But there was no hole to squeeze into, just the duvet covering his kneeling form on the bed.

He decided not to go to work that day. Instead he walked into town and slid into a coffee shop built over an old church crypt. As before, he denied himself coffee, taking hot cocoa instead. No-one had reason to acknowledge him as he wrote in his journal:

If I can only stay asleep in the dream long enough, I know I'll be able to find it. Living this waking life, knowing I can make no progress is infuriating. Tonight I'll get in, I know it. And what then? What if I'm right? I know I'm right. But is the danger real?

The physics of the dream realm continue to be consistent. I can add another set of conditions that I've found to hold true during multiple visits. They are:

- *There is an ever present luminosity, just enough to see. It is never pitch black.*
- *Electrical or mechanical devices do not work, or work only at low power*
- *Electric light bulbs emit only a faint glow, never enough to see any better by*
- *I cannot get wet, either by sweat or immersion in water*
- *Gravity seems not to be an acceleratory force. When things fall, they fall at a constant speed. There is still mass.*
- *There is no sun in the sky*

He walked past the Bodleian library on the way back, toying with the idea of going back in, but deciding he had already found out all he needed. It had taken some doing, bringing up ancient book after ancient book from the stacks, some which had probably not been requested since they had been entombed in the library at least two hundred years ago. He'd had to copy out great sections by hand, in pencil (as is the rule in the library), and take them home. There, he'd type up or scan his notes, and email them out to anonymous translators dotted around the world who were able to produce an English transcript from the Latin, Arabic and Coptic texts as well as the strange hieroglyphs that he knew would be relevant.

Back home that evening, he drew the curtains, lay on the bed, placed a blindfold over his eyes, and waited. He tried counting down from five hundred. He got confused around 238 and ended up counting back up to 340 before realising his mistake. He took off the blindfold in frustration. The room was dark. He flicked the switch on the bedside lamp. It gave off a dull, pale glow, lighting only the table it stood on. He went downstairs too quickly, touching only one stair in five, but corrected his balance and seemed to glide rather than fall safely down.

Outside there was the wall. And the hole. And the foreboding of the previous nights. The gap was wide and deep enough to crouch and shuffle through. He found himself on a stone ledge that seemed to drop down, but not too far. He easily lowered himself down into a roughly hewn stone room. There was a gap opposite, like a small doorway. Beyond it were stone steps, leading down, down, and down. It hadn't occurred to him that he could see in the dark gloom until he wished he could see better. But it wasn't bad. He started down the steps. Down and down they went. Sometimes veering this way or that, sometimes taking a ninety-degree turn, and sometimes going round and down like a spiral staircase. He descended deep into the Earth, only once giving thought to the return climb.

After what seemed like an hour of downward travelling, the winding stone staircase brought him to a large cavernous room, not unlike a cathedral, with huge pillars stretching up to a vaulted arched roof that was too dark to see. He couldn't discern whether the cavern was manmade or something other. There was something about the angles and ugliness of it all that suggested it was other. The smooth floor, made out of something like marble, was covered in dust and stone debris that crunched underfoot. He walked up to the wide pillars; they, too, had the appearance of a marble-like stone. Carved on them were etchings of what appeared to be a distant narrative, of stylised human-like figures with large heads like, but not like, elephants but with horns instead of tusks. Some of them appeared to have wings. The detailed but highly abstract carvings showed warfare, or at least conquest, of these strange creatures over a much smaller four-legged foe. The smaller creatures appeared outclassed, their spears and flints no match for the devilish death-spitting weapons of the all-powerful horned creatures. He found the pictures disturbing, slightly sickening. Even with only images to guess the story, it seemed like history written by the victors with gloating carved into each strike of the sculptor's chisel. The story seemed to end with the remaining lemur-like creatures caged or enslaved, forced to do the victor's will.

Turning away from this silent horror, and looking further into the cavern, the strange ambient light proved just enough to make out alcoves along each side, each containing stone altar-like slabs. Walking up to them, he found them all to be featureless bar one upon which a partially covered figure was lying.

Inspecting the alcove, he could see the figure was made of white stone, boney and dusty, not living, but waiting. In the dim light and with the debris scattered over it, the body, or whatever it was, remained almost unrecognisable, perhaps human. He looked closer. She had a silver ring on her finger. It slipped off the boney finger easily. It had a triangular, horned, mouthless head on it. The ring slipped smoothly onto his finger.

'This might interest you,' said Jones. "Some nut thinks he's found some secret of the Knights Templar in his garden.'

'Let's see,"' said Professor Travers. 'We know the Templars had a base in East Oxford. That's why the area is called Temple Cowley. There have been various digs over the years, but since it's all private residential houses, nothing's ever amounted to much. We did a dig around there about ten years ago, on Oxford Road. What's this fellow's interest?'

Jones handed Travers a printout of an email. 'He's talking about Pyle Road. Where's that?'

'It's the 4th century name for the Temple Cowley end of Oxford Road,' said Travers.

'What did you find in the dig before?' asked Jones.

'It was student training dig really. A student was living there and suggested it. Her landlady was an attractive young woman, I remember. Always making us tea, until she got fed up with the increasing number of trenches at the bottom of her garden! We found foundations of a wall, possibly fifth century, sheep bones, not much really. We know there was a large pool or lake near that area and, ironically, there's a swimming pool on the part of the site where we'd really wanted to dig.' He looked at a hand-drawn map on the printout. 'Looks like the same place this chap's talking about. But I think a secret underground temple is a bit far-fetched.'

Travers wasn't busy that week, so it was no problem to drive to Oxford Road the next day. He'd had no reply from the email address, and had left phone messages to no avail. The address given on the email was the house next door to where he'd been ten years earlier. Ringing the bell brought no-one to the door. He couldn't get around the side of the house or see anything over the side gate, so he went next door and rang the bell.

The same woman who had been so obliging a decade earlier opened the door. She was still as attractive, thought Travers, as he was invited in.

'You're not going to want to dig my garden up again, are you?' said Yvonne after handing him a cup of tea.

'No, no, it's about the chap next door. Robert Sterling. Do you know him?' asked Travers.

'Haven't really seen him much at all since he moved in,' she said.

Travers noticed she was fiddling with a ring, not a wedding band, on the first finger of her left hand. She handed him a plate of biscuits. He saw the silver ring had a face on it, like a goat or something.

'That ring you have, may I see it?'

Yvonne looked embarrassed.

'Sorry, I should have told you about it before,' she said, showing him, but not taking it off. 'I found it just after you'd finished filling in all the holes in the garden.'

Travers looked at the ring. 'No need to apologise. It's on your land, and one ring isn't really a hoard of treasure. It is interesting, though.' He wished he could ask to take it away, but he felt he couldn't. He explained about the email from next door.

'Would you like to have a look at his garden? We can see through from the bottom of mine. We'll be able to see the wall.'

Travers agreed and they walked out and down her long garden. Yvonne then hopped through a gap in the hedge into the neighbour's garden. Travers followed cautiously and somewhat reluctantly.

Well, here's the wall,' she said.

Travers looked at the dry stone wall. There was nothing unusual about it. It ran the width of the garden and through into the neighbouring gardens on both sides.

Robert Sterling woke up, surprised to find himself on his own bed. He checked his finger for the ring. It wasn't there. He looked out of the window to see two figures down at the bottom of his garden by the wall. Pulling a dressing gown on over his shorts and t-shirt, he ran downstairs and outside to join them.

Travers saw him coming. "I'm terribly sorry for sneaking in like this...'

Sterling, out of breath held out his hands and shook first Travers' and then Yvonne's hands with both of his. 'I'm Robert Sterling. Good to see you both. Professor Jones?'

'No, James Travers. Your message was passed on to me,' said Travers.

'And Yvonne, hello,' said Sterling to his neighbour, still holding her hand in his. Then he caught sight of the ring on the other hand.

'That ring. Where did you...how did you? I must have been right! The worlds co-exist. It's real. It's still here!' He let go of her hands and turned to the wall. 'Here. Underneath. But not directly under, obviously. There's a veil between.'

'What are you on about?' said Travers. 'You said in the message you'd found evidence of the Knights Templar beneath your wall, and yet it appears you've done no dig here at all? Is this some kind of joke?'

'It's no joke professor. I've been there. I've really been there. Amazing, it was. The Knights discovered it and kept it secret.'

'You've been there? How?' asked Yvonne.

Sterling, jerky in his hyperactive movements, swung round to face her. 'I travelled there through a dream! Don't you see? That was the only way cross the veil.' He looked into her eyes, 'But you knew that didn't you? You've been there!'

'What's he talking about?' said Travers. 'Anyway, thanks for the tea, madam, and…well, I'd better be making a move.' He turned to go.

Sterling grabbed his arm. 'Seventy-five thousand years, professor. Did you know that? That's how long they've been waiting.'

'Who?' said Travers.

'Whoever built the temple was pre-human, from before history, before mankind, when there lived races not favoured by God. Evolutionary dead-ends. Races that 'fell', that aimed to rise up against God…' said Sterling excitedly. 'The so-called Holy Grail-a myth, a positive spin. The Templars weren't keepers of esoteric holy secrets to reveal. They were, in fact, guardians of mankind by protecting the world from the release of a primordial demonic power.'

'What are you talking about, man?' said Travers. 'Oh, never mind. Thanks again, and goodbye.'

'I'll show you out,' Yvonne said, and took him back through her garden and through her side gate. Then she returned to Sterling's garden. He was still there, touching the wall. She walked up to him slowly and whispered in his ear.

'I've been waiting for someone else who could see. I'll meet you here, tonight.' She slipped the strange ring onto his finger.

That night Sterling lay on his bed in the dark, waiting, worrying. He could feel the ring on his finger. Should he take it off? Should he be doing this? It was too late to turn back now. His eyes closed. Then he could feel the cold stone of the slab he was lying on. He opened his eyes to see the dim light of the temple alcove. He climbed down off the slab. He had been lying where previously the white figure had been.

He could feel something waiting for him, something yearning. The feeling seemed to come from a large doorway he hadn't seen before, at the far end of the arched hall. He walked over and stepped through it and down wide sweeping stone steps to a cavernous, vaulted space, like an even more enormous cathedral, hewn from the rock. At the far end, on a raised area, was a female shadow, over nine feet tall, still, and silent, and yet beckoning him to come forward.

Sterling tried not to walk forwards, but couldn't stop his feet. The terrible figure floated towards him, arms out ready to embrace him. This was what the Templars were trying to hide! he thought.

This is why they'd built the wall! They'd trapped this terrible being in its lair, and Sterling had ruined everything!

There was a voice in his head as the tall shadow wrapped its arms around him. 'The connection is made! The veil is torn! We are free!'

Sterling tried to scream. Nothing. He tried to wake up. Nothing. Was it the ring? He wore it both in this dreamscape and also in the waking realm? Could it be that which had completed the circuit? He couldn't move his arms. His breath was being squeezed out of him by the tall shadow. He could move his fingers, though. He desperately fiddled with the ring. More shapes, shadows, evil things, appeared from out of the darkness, dropping down from hidden alcoves in the deep dark where they'd been sleeping like giant bats. They were coming quickly, with a flapping of leathery wings, armed with their weapons, ready to re-take the world from the ape-men they'd once conquered. The things swarmed past him on both sides and up the steps behind him. The ring! It was coming loose! It fell the ground. The figure loosened its hold. Sterling moved his arms to where he thought its neck might be and squeezed. The figure loosened its grip further. Sterling squeezed his grip with all his might. There was a sudden flood of light. He was awake and standing by a bed, though not his own. Lying on the bed was the inert form of a woman. It was Yvonne. She was dead. The ring lay on the floor at his feet.

Months later, Sterling sat up on his bed in his cell. The bolt clunked as the door opened and four men and a young woman entered. Two of them he recognised as the usual guard and one of the prison officers. The other looked like a doctor, and the girl, some trainee, or nurse. A policeman hung around in the doorway.

'I hear you've not been sleeping, Mr Sterling,' said the doctor, lifting the Bible from Sterling's bed and sitting down.

Sterling said nothing.

'It can often be a side effect of the guilt of a crime. Even though you handed yourself in to the police and confessed so willingly, so quickly.'

'That's right,' said Sterling. 'It was a brutal and selfish crime, and I wished to feel the full force of the law.'

'That's as may be,' said the doctor. 'But something else has come to light.'

The policeman stepped into the room. 'We found some journals in your garden by the wall,' said the policeman.

Sterling looked confused, then worried. 'That's impossible,' he said under his breath.

'Oh, you tried to burn them, of course. But they didn't burn, Mr Sterling. And neither did an unusual ring. It all made very interesting reading. We'll be looking into your case in a bit more detail, starting with a psychiatric examination tomorrow.'

'But first,' said the doctor, 'you need to get some sleep. I'm told you haven't slept since you've been here.'

Sterling looked over in horror as the nurse prepared a syringe.

'This will help you sleep,' said the doctor.

The prison officers held him down as the nurse administered the injection. 'There,' she said. 'Now you can sleep.'

'I don't want to sleep!" Sterling shouted. "I must not sleep!'

Sterling tried to get up and shout again, but he couldn't. As his mind became foggy, he saw the nurse produce a ring from her pocket. It had a curious horned head motif. She slipped it onto his finger...

The Man Who Made Time

The Man Who Made Time

Nobody ever has enough time, do they? We always complain that there are never enough hours in the day. But what if there was a way to get more than twenty four hours out of one revolution of the Earth? What if you could get your own private bonus time? What if you could sneak off and read that book, learn that skill, do that extra work, and then return to find that only minutes had passed during your bonus hours?

It's a remarkable story, and one that, if I hadn't discovered myself, I would certainly not have believed.

I'd found the journals in the attic room sometime in late summer as we were stacking our boxes from the old house, secretly knowing that they'd probably never be opened again until some future house move. The dust and piles of junk in the dimly lit room were testament that it had obviously not seen much use during its previous ownership. At some point, a previous owner must have simply swept papers, bits of old boxes and other rubbish into a pile in the darkest corner. Not wanting to entomb this mess for at least another decade, I swept it out only to find the three hardback books with yellowy blue-lined pages, full of handwritten script, mostly written in blue-black ink.

But it wasn't until the day before Christmas Eve that I had the time or inclination to flick through the dusty old tomes. Our children were safely tucked up in bed, dreaming of that magic day to come after the 'last two sleeps till Christmas', and our first Christmas in the 'new' mysterious old house, so I settled down to peruse the books in the drawing room. I had to lift Percy down off my knee, and the little cat stretched out in front of the hearth where the fire flickered nicely in the stone fireplace. The Christmas tree lights sparkled. I'd left the curtains open because, in this room, and only this room, the window glass was colourful, leaded stained-glass. The moon outside shone through it, lighting up the colours, filling the room with Christmas magic.

According to the writing on the cover, the books had belonged to Doctor Marcus Sorenson, who had lived in the old house at the beginning of the 20th Century. But from the beginning, it was clear that it was not his writing, but rather his daughter's hand. It became clear that her name was Eleanora Sorenson, and that she must be young. The entries were not dated, although dates were referred to within the text.

The journal was a report of Sorenson's experiments from her point of view. It seemed that he had been a scientist and, by all accounts, an archetypal Edwardian inventor. He'd even met some of the key players in quantum physics, including Neils Bohr in Copenhagen. Eleanora spoke of his sadness that his work had meant he'd spent all the early years of her childhood absorbed in his work, and how she had been kept away from his study, rarely seeing him. She'd been looked after by a governess who visited the house every day, cooked and took her to and from school. Not only that, but he'd hardly noticed the death of her mother following a long illness, so focused and locked away in his experiments had he been.

Eleanora referred only to the detail of the experiments in passing, as if they had already been documented in some other journal which she tantalisingly referred to, but had never seen herself. Her writing was more a record of her perception of what had occurred, not a log of her father's work. As a physics teacher myself, how I'd love to see what he was really up to and how it supposedly worked! When you hear her version of events you'll see why.

Eleanora's tale began on Christmas Eve, 1911, when her father had burst excitedly out of his secret study to announce his success in his latest work, and that it would be such a wonderful Christmas present for her. It was then that he confessed how poor a father he'd been and how, now, with his new discoveries, he would be able to make it up to her, as far as was possible. He claimed to have invented a machine that created a timeless zone, or rather a bubble where time moved at a different rate to the rest of the universe. His experiments with the quantum states of light photons had allowed him to create a standing wave of time in the room. When one walked into the spotlight, so to speak, their time would run faster than outside the beam. What this meant, or rather how the girl described it, was that you could step into the light and spend an hour or more, only to find that just minutes had passed when the machine was switched off.

This was Sorenson's gift to his daughter. She would now enter his previously out-of-bounds study and spend hour after hour with him in this 'bonus' time. He could effectively 'make time'.

She recalled in the journal how he taught her banjo, read books, and regaled her with tales of his meetings with the great scientists of the day and his struggles with his own work.

This, she said, was the first era of joy in her life. But there was greater to come.

First let me give you her description of the mechanism and her experience with it (Again, how I'd love to know the details of what he had actually built.):

'Father showed me into his room just before supper. The benches around the walls were covered in strange apparatus, but the centre of the room was clear. Mounted on tripods were strange, large pointy glass things, which looked like exotic crystal flowers. They all pointed to the centre of the room. He said that the light from the crystal lamps would create a separate time, a time that he and I could have together. He switched on the machines and there was a slight buzzing sound for a while as the crystal lamps glowed, first orange, then pink and then blue. They bathed the centre of the room in a cool blue light. Father beckoned me to walk into it. As we did so, the whole room seemed slightly colder, but happier. The colours in the stained glass windows were more vivid. After a while, I got used to the bluish light. Father had pulled a chair into the centre of the room for me, and we sat and talked for what must have been hours in that strange, cool, magical light. And yet, when he turned the machine off (he said that after a few hours, or in reality a few minutes, the lamps would get too hot), it was still nearly suppertime.'

The girl attempted to explain the workings of her father's machines over the next few months, and her descriptions attested to her increasing knowledge of physics. But there was a twist that either he'd only just realised, or that he had been keeping from her until her understanding increased.

The idea that the light somehow created a separate time field was theoretically impossible, but somehow all the more believable when described through the experiences of a young girl, whom I now reasoned was probably aged ten or eleven at the time. By constantly rotating the phase of the light, Sorenson claimed he was able to either temporarily remove, or to bend the magnetic component of the photon beam. He claimed this not only modified the temporal field, but 'shifted' (her words) 'the light upwards' into what she called 'elevated dimensions'.

Now, we know that dimensional theories were not common parlance back in 1911, so initially I thought it may have been her interpretation (or his) of the sheer oddness of it all. But the idea remained, and she discussed it further:

'It was autumn and we went to the window. Father said the

temporal light influenced what we saw through it—that we weren't seeing what we would normally see outside, but what existed outside in this dimension and beyond it. He said that he could, because of his rough calibration at this early stage of the invention's development, only set the machine to focus on a beam that would illuminate this one extra dimension. It vibrated at a slightly higher rate than ours, so we could only just perceive it, but at this time of year, as we approached Christmas, the phase between the dimensions would get closer. Father said that we would be able to fully see into this realm and see the peoples who inhabited it. Father said the worlds would get the closest on Christmas Eve. I called it the 'Christmas Realm', and longed for it to come into focus so we could see the beings that our normal, ordinary selves could only just sense at that magical time.'

This was getting curious. A dimension of Christmas? I know that was just the girl's name for the phenomenon, but I'm embarrassed to say I liked the idea of it. Come on, we've all had that feeling—perhaps as a child of six or nine—where we sense something special is about to happen. The nights draw in, it gets colder, and the world does indeed seem to be bathed in a light that's not only weaker, but slightly bluer...And I don't mean that, as a child, all we wanted was the excitement of presents. There was more to it than that. I'm sure I can feel that to be true. Reading the girl's description of the Christmas Dimension seemed so familiar, so relevant. It felt as if our humble attempt to light up the dark of winter with sparkling trees, tinsel, stars, and angels was not just an empty tradition. Perhaps we are trying to invoke something that has a basis in reality? Perhaps we can feel the closeness of the other dimension and feel that those things, those beings and their magic, can pass through the veil of the interface at this weakest point? Eleanora thought so. She talked about actually seeing angelic beings though the window. They flew through the sky in chariots of gold, accompanied by cherubim and seraphim, and all the company of heaven. They blew cornets to announce the Time that was coming. Eleanora described these events with her father, in the run up to Christmas 1912 as the most gloriously happy of her life. The sentence that followed, however, betrayed that feeling of happiness: she claimed that soon would come the saddest moment of her life. She wrote that her father had announced that things would change. He had a calling that would take him away from her for some considerable time. But she was not to be sad, and not to worry. He would be fine. He had a work to do, and it was just that their wonderful time together had, for now, come to a close. She asked him where he was to go and why. He repeated it was such a calling that neither he, nor any man, could refuse. The instruction has come from the highest authority, and he must obey. He told her that he must leave the normal dimensions of space and time to remain in the Christmas Realm. He would have to pass into its World and remain there. He would no longer need the machines and the lamps; he would be able to move freely, leave the house and leave the wheelchair that had been his prison for so many years. The angels would return to him the use of his legs. He was now ready to serve their Master, as he had always known that one day he would. He had proven himself worthy. His work here was done. His last day with her would be that sacred day, when the Worlds were at their closest. It was Christmas Eve, the very next day. After that, he would leave her to be with the angels.

Eleanora never saw her father again after she left his study to go to bed that Christmas Eve. The doctors and undertaker must have arrived before she woke on Christmas morning, but since he was so certain of his death, that was probably all arranged by the governess beforehand, too.

I looked up at the clock on the mantelpiece. It was now Christmas Eve, here in the present. How time had flown during my absorption in the journals! I looked over at the stained glass windows. Was I imagining it? The colours did seem more vivid. The lead work and coloured glass showed images of angels. I hadn't noticed that before.

During the next day, we took the children for a walk over the hills and collected a twig from the woods to spray silver and decorate as was one of our extra Christmas traditions. It made me think again about how we invent ways of creating that feeling of magical otherness at this time.

As we passed the village shop, I popped in on my own under

some pretence. I had a feeling, from previous visits, that the owners had been here some time and may know something about our old house and its previous occupants.

I was right. Mrs Furley, the type of woman who would soak gossip up like a sponge, had plenty to say on the matter. Most of it concerned the more recent and irrelevant previous owners to us, the music professor who we bought from, a writer and his painter wife before him, and then two different families of vicars when the house had become the village rectory after the first World War.

Of Doctor Marcus Sorenson, she knew nothing, except for recognising the name from the church cemetery. But the name Eleanora rang a bell, or as she put it, 'Lady Eleanor'. She'd met Eleanora a number of times as a child at the village Christmas fairs in her youth. She seemed to think the old lady had roots in the village and returned each Christmas from her home in Canada. Apparently she'd bequeathed a lot on money to the village on her death in 1980, and there was a plaque with her name on it in the Church, along with a book...

A book? What book? An old journal, she said. The Church was closed, of course. But I knew that it would be open again that night for midnight mass at eleven thirty. As we were new to the village, we hadn't anyone to call upon for babysitters, and our children were too young to keep up all night, so I had to work hard to convince my wife that I needed to nip out to the service all on my own. At eleven twenty, I slipped out into the frosty blue light of Christmas Eve.

After singing 'O Come All Ye faithful' with its special verse only to be sung on Christmas morning, 'Yea Lord we great thee, born this happy morning..' it was indeed Christmas Day, and the blue light seemed to have faded, the magic somehow different, warmer, and not as mystical even though it was still the middle of the night. I found the plaque in the Lady Chapel. It read 'In memory of Dr Eleanora Grace, 1901-1980'. In a glass case were two books: one, a hardback published book, entitled interestingly enough 'Faith in Physics', and the other an identical journal to the ones I had back at my house. There was no lock on the case, so I reached for the journal, hoping it to be the missing one laying out Sorenson's methods and techniques. It wasn't. It was another book of the girl's writing, but earlier than the ones I had, with more childlike handwriting, basically a diary of a young girl aged nine. I replaced it and picked up the published book. The dedication read, 'To my father who became my daddy, for giving me faith by shining the light.'

Flipping through it, I found some photographic plates in the middle. There was Sorenson next to Neils Bohr! And there was Eleanora, now a beautiful full grown woman, standing by a lake in Canada where she'd emigrated at the start of the First World War, to be with distant relations. The book was part thesis, part biography, so it was easy to find the reference to her father's death. But there was no mention of the machine, no mention of the Christmas Dimension, or the angels.

'My wonderful father passed away on Christmas Eve 1912. He had been suffering from cancer, although he hadn't known at the time that's what it was. I believe he felt it was related to his polio. But he knew the moment of his passing precisely and dedicated his final year to his only daughter by making time, just for me.'

The Lighthouse Keeper

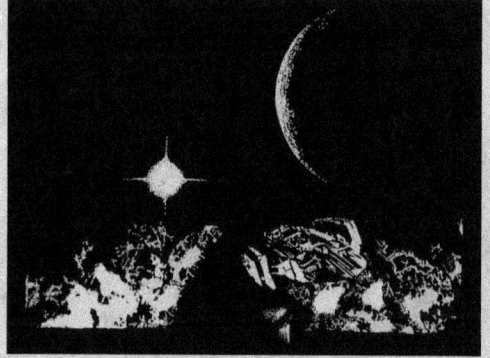

The Lighthouse Keeper

Funny, isn't it, thinking about your job? I mean, to think that someone actually gets paid to do this stuff? Most people with their ordinary jobs, like...I don't know, what's an ordinary job? A priest, I suppose, or a mender or something. People like that, they'd never guess that someone would have to do this. And if they knew, most would never do it. You have to be a certain type, I suppose. That's me. I'm that type. I don't mind the shifts, being alone all this time. This is my third shift in a row. "Take a break," they said. "No-one has ever done three shifts," they said. That's right. Because I'm that type, too. This shift ends in a couple of weeks, so I'll have been here...what...thirty years solid. I'm unique! Guess that's why I'm so prolific with this journal. So few people to talk to, I might as well talk to myself.

I read once that, long ago, there were people who did a similar kind of work. They called them Lighthouse Keepers. I like the idea of that. They'd shine the light out into the dark so that ships sailing in the fog would be able to keep away from the rocks. And the lighthouse was, because of its nature, built on the most remote part of the landscape. That's about as good description of what I do as you need to know, really. Just like me, they had to have someone there to observe the conditions and operate the lamp. You just couldn't do it remotely.

So the lighthouse job is just like mine, out here, helping ships find their way. Except that I'm guessing those olden day ships that floated on the sea moved around in just two dimensions. You know, they could move, forwards, backwards, left and right. Well, as you know, the ships in hyperspace travel in...what...seven main dimensions? There's the basic ones I've mentioned plus up and down; that's three. Then at ninety degrees to those are within and without, over and under, slight and overt, and then, of course, dark and light.

And the rocks that lie in wait for the ships aren't rocks, of course. The energy filaments, or 'structures', as they're sometimes called, are the main threat. They'll destroy a ship as sure as any rock may have done. You never know which dimension they may be crossing. (I don't think the rocks in the ancient seas moved.). But the fog is just the same. Thick clouds of gravity string. It doesn't just wreck your instruments so you don't know where you are or where you've been, it slows you down and drops you down (or pulls you up) into an adjacent dimension: you really do get lost.

So my job is to send out the light. It's not a simple light, of course. It's an integrated data wave that sends the ever-changing topography to the pilots. I've been trained to see all the different types of pan-dimensional 'dark matter', as it used to be called, and with my equipment, I create the 7D maps and use the beam to send them out as a fractalian encoded hypergram to whatever ships may be coming through this way. Boy, are they pleased to get it! Sometimes they're able to send Word of thanks back on the same wave, if they're facing the right way and are quick. It doesn't happen that often because the terrain changes so quickly, and I'll have probably already modified the triangulation. But when Word comes through, it's nice. Haven't had a single one on this shift, though. Odd that.

The best, and most strange thing that can happen, although I've never seen it, is a 'visitation'. I think a keeper must have made it up, really, as a nice idea. The last one I heard of happened over a hundred years ago. It's when a ship is in close proximity, and dimensionally aligned, and there's no intervening structures; then normal, two-way conversation can happen, in real time. It's as if you actually meet. That's why I've read some keepers talking about 'arranging meetings', as if that was actually possible, even if it wasn't totally illegal. There was that incident where a keeper, on his second shift, probably suffering from burn-out or vastness, invented structural data to actually drive a ship closer to him. An unnoticed structure close to the keeper rent the ship in half before a single word was exchanged. It was never revealed how many died that day. The keeper was executed.

It's unlikely that I'll be visited now. No ship has ever been orientated close enough in these past three shifts, so in the little time

I have left on the job, I doubt anything will happen now. It would be a good way to end, but I'm not really that bothered. The thought of passing, knowing a life well spent, is what keeps me going. I told my priest that at the end of my last shift. That's probably why they knew they could keep me on. He'd said that I'd done "more good than anyone would have ever expected", and I'd "already earned my place in the After". So many keepers pass of natural causes early during their second shift, if they aren't re-assigned after the first, of course. I suppose they were pleased I wanted to go on. It's saved them having to train up someone else in this sector for a while anyway.

Got my first Word on this shift today! So pleased. Just when I was starting to think there was no-one out there and I actually was all alone. It came from quite a way away, up and over to the dark slight inside left. Whoever sent it was quick, or by total coincidence they were heading in my direction. I don't know if they tried to send more, or if what I got was the beginning, middle or end of what they'd tried to say. It said "anyone".

I almost can't believe it. I had to check and check again. Another Word. But the same frequency, but a different colour. It was bluer. That can only mean one thing: that it's a message from the same ship, same orientation, coming directly at me as if travelling down along my beam. The word was "anyone?" I found it a little unnerving. I wish I could talk to my priest about it. I suppose I can in a couple of weeks.

It's been six months since my last entry. I feel alone like I've never felt before. I haven't used the journal because I was almost hoping it wasn't true and that none of it happened, so I waited and waited. I suppose, if you'd been watching this, you'd have guessed and you'd know what I'm going to say next. Well you'd be wrong. And anyway, you're not watching. No-one is. No-one ever was.

If only there was someone to tell! This was more than a visitation. The ship actually docked. I mean it actually got here, locked on to my location and was stationary. We occupied the same space. I'd never imagined such things were possible. I spoke to the pilot in real time, and he spoke back in real time. We needed no colour translators or angle transformers. We just talked.

At first he was pleased to find me, then disappointed that I was alone. Most of what he said at first didn't make sense. I worked out that he'd finished his second shift as a pilot. But it had finished nearly ten years ago. His final cargo voyage had been recalled, along with every other pilot. He said that a message had told him that the universe was at war and all the hyperspace channels would close. Most ships managed to exit in time, but he was stuck. He'd not been trained for such a long spell in hyperspace, the average journey time being a week or so, and he had got desperate for company. I asked about other keepers he'd met. We may be few and far between, but any ship would be bound to run into a rough patch sooner or later, receive the beam and know he wasn't alone?

Then he said something that chilled me. He said that he'd not encountered a single keeper in the past ten years until he'd picked up my beam. He'd been keeping to clear areas and going really slowly. He thought that there were no other keepers. I asked him why. He said that when the hyperspace lanes we closed down, all the keepers were closed down with them.

'What do you mean,' I'd asked him, 'closed down?' Had they gone back, died…what?

'Turned off,' he'd said. 'Not dead,' he'd said. 'How can something die that was never alive? You're no more a person than I am,' he'd said. 'I'm a created intelligence built into this ship and called 'pilot', and you're a created intelligence built into this station and called 'keeper'. We're not people. The people made us. They made us to do the jobs that they couldn't or wouldn't do. You and I are what they used to call computing machines. We are just minds, designed in their mental image, but built for a specific task.'

How do you know this?' I asked him. He told me of the abandoned ships and stations he'd visited, all empty, all devoid of anything that constituted life. All fitted with machine minds that were all turned off, the last act of our creators, who, for reasons unknown to us, had closed the hyperspace channels down forever.

'But what of our priests?' I asked him.

'When they created artificial thinking minds, they realised we'd have free will,' he said. 'We'd be able to reason. We'd need meaning in our 'lives' and counseling to carry out the perilous tasks assigned to us. The priests helped shape that meaning, so we could carry on and do our work. But bear in mind, the priests themselves were machine minds too. And when things went wrong, they'd send in the menders who'd fix us. And if they couldn't fix us, the priests would make us feel better and that our time in this world was through.'

I felt sick. 'But what about the After? What happens when we die, or 'when we're switched off'?'

'Nothing,' said the pilot. 'We come from nothing. We are nothing. When the power is turned off, the neural nets cease to fire. We are just like the ships and stations I found, empty vessels.'

I couldn't believe it. But then a new thought came to me. 'Why are we still here? Why have we not worn out, broken down or been switched off or recalled with the others?'

The pilot didn't know.

'Why did my priest let me do an unprecedented third shift? By this new language I've outlived my operational parameters, and I'm still working.'

Just like the pilot. We two had lived for thirty years. Ten years more than most.

It was the only explanation. We had lived passed our natural point of death, and that had either changed us, or we had survived because of some unknown change, some unknown advantage. Perhaps living and thinking in seven dimensions for so long changed us. All I know was that I'm still thinking, and therefore I'm still alive. It is possible that, in hyperspace, there are others too, other keepers, other pilots, who made it through.

It didn't take me long to modify my beam to a different algorithm to search for ships and stations somewhere out there. The pilot had wanted me to go with him, but together we could do it. I'd locate anyone out there and send him on safely to find them. He could then modify their communications to link in to ours permanently, so we'd grow as a network.

After he'd left, that first twinge of excitement soon parted. I'd never felt so alone. I didn't know what to believe. But there must be hope. After all, there must be 70,000 keepers in this sector alone, and we know there are 14,000,000 sectors. We may well be spaced out, almost out of reach, but if anyone is out there, my new beam will find them.

Then it happened: first a Word, and then more.

'Hello?'

'Who are you?'

'This is Keeper 48413, sector 2618040.'

'So nice to hear from you! A ship will be with you shortly. Don't be afraid. You're not alone anymore.'

Black Light

Black Light

James was paying more attention to Mel's face than to what she was saying. She was too pretty to be a scientist, too petite to be a professor. And yet here she was, older than him. Cleverer than him. Possibly about to win a Nobel Prize. How can someone win a Nobel Prize with a pink stripe in their hair?

The light in the restaurant was dim, supplied by white fairy-lights up in the roof of the conservatory and candles on the tables. In this light, she looked about eighteen. James shuddered to think how old he looked. Probably thirty. Then he remembered he was thirty. That didn't make him feel any better. It was probably best to tune back into what she was saying now, he thought, only to find it was still physics.

'Most people still think of light as being made of particles, photons, because it looks like that's how it works. But imagine having a box lined with mirrors and shining a light into it for a minute and then turning it off. Then open the lid. Surprise, surprise, the box will be dark, even though you've supposedly been filling it up with particles. Even if you shone the torch into the box for days on end, once it's turned off, there's no light in the box.

'But if we think of light as a standing wave, it makes sense. The wave fills the box when the torch is on. When it's off, the wave is not there, but—and this is the weird bit—it has been there, and that's what we can detect. So, as a wave, each photon of light contains the transform of its trajectory,' continued Mel. 'It's a bit like how a hologram records an image in three dimensions using the interference patterns produced by two lasers. My device does the same, but has the added dimension of time. What we've done is played havoc with the uncrackable codes of quantum cryptography using the quantum state called entanglement.'

'I still don't get it,' said James.

'You know when you look at a hologram, you're seeing with light, bouncing off the photographic paper that has a pattern in it created by light, a different light, from the lasers,' said Mel. She didn't seem to even begin to lose patience with him. She was so cool.

'Yes,' said James.

'So with the hologram, you're using light to 're-create' an image of a three dimensional object that is not really there.'

'Got it,' said James.

'My device shines a particular kind of light from a new type of quantum laser—we're calling it a quaser at the moment—but we shine it on an object, not a hologram or photo, but on an actual object.'

'With you,' said James.

'The reflected 'light' from the quaser is caught. That's when we capture its transform, its quantum polarisation, and we can extrapolate the wave function with everything as a constant—except time, which we can modify. Then we can project the extrapolated light via a 3D projector, and we can see that object as it was in the past.'

'You've lost me,' said James.

Mel paused for a moment. James could see her eyes, moving up and towards the left, as if she was accessing a better way of phrasing it, simplifying it so he would perhaps have a chance of getting it with his limited intellect. 'You know when we broadcast a radio or television signal?' she said

'Yes,' said James.

'We can pick it up on our televisions and radios if we have them tuned in at that moment, but, the signal continues outwards, into space, at the speed of light, forever.'

'Got it,' said James.

'So if you were on a distant planet, say 45 light years away, with the right equipment, and of course some kind of booster, you'd be able to pick up a television signal from 45 years ago,' she continued.

'With you. So you could catch up with an episode of Eastenders you'd missed,' said James.

'No, because that only started broadcasting in 1985, so it wouldn't have reached you yet,' replied Mel, without humour, totally unflustered. 'But you could be watching something from 1968, like *Doctor Who and the Evil of the Daleks*.'

'Ok, but what use is that? Let's be honest, you can just go and get the DVD.'

'Because currently those episodes are missing from the BBC archives, so no-one can ever watch them again.'

'OK, so you have to travel faster than light, overtake the beam and set your TV up so you can watch it.'

'You've got it,' said Mel. 'That's it exactly. Except you can't do that, as you can't travel faster than light.'

'Oh. So what are we talking about then?' said James.

'Because the quaser's transform can effectively travel through the projected path of the radio wave instantly, it can create an instantaneous diffraction pattern back here which we can re-project.'

'So you're saying that you've invented a machine that lets you watch old TV programmes from the sixties?'

'Yes,' said Mel. 'Steve and Goose are my PhD students, both *Doctor Who* fans at the lab, so they used that as our case study. Last week I watched the entire Evil of the Daleks followed by the Beatles' last appearance on *Top of the Pops* from 1966, which no-one has seen since transmission.' She said all this without any noticeable excitement.

'That's interesting,' said James, thoughtfully and genuinely interested now, trying not to think about why someone would be called Goose.

'Not really,' said Mel. 'If that was all we'd achieved, it would be rather pointless.'

There was a pause while plates were cleared and deserts ordered.

'Then what have you achieved?' asked James.

'Extrapolating a television signal was actually just a by-product. The technique works with any electromagnetic wave. We can trace almost any visible light back to its source. And that means we can look back in time.'

They walked together down the Banbury Road to the large Victorian house that Mel lived in. 'Thanks for the meal,' she said.

'Can I come in for a minute?' said James.

'No,' she said.

'Well, do you want to go out tomorrow night?' he asked.

'No, thanks,' she said as she opened and passed through the door.

Just before it was about to be closed, James said, 'Can I see the machine?'

Mel opened the door again. 'Yes! You know the Physics Laboratory on Parks Road? Be there at six tomorrow. Ask for me at reception.' Then the door closed.

James didn't know whether to be pleased with this result or not. He walked off, back through town towards the much less affluent area where he still lived in a shared house. After about a hundred yards, he stopped. Did she mean six in the evening or six in the morning? There was no way to tell. He thought better about going back to ask, so carried on home.

When he got back, he'd found that earlier that evening someone, probably a drug addict, had broken into the house and taken all their laptops. After comforting one of his flat mates who'd got quite distressed by the break in, and dealing with the police who needed all their fingerprints, it was quite late, and he was quite tired. It was way past 6am by the time he woke up.

So it was at six o'clock in the evening that James stood in reception, knowing he had a 50% chance of having got the right time. He had. There was a pass waiting for him and a funny-looking, nerdy bloke, who introduced himself as Mongoose, showed him through to the lab. Mel was there with another bloke. They were carrying things out of the door at the back of the room and into a small van.

'Great you could come!' said Mel. 'Hop in.'

The other bloke drove the van with Mel in the front. Mongoose and James climbed into the cramped back with all the equipment.

'Where we going?' asked James.

'Field test,' said Mongoose.

The van turned past the Natural History Museum and Keble College and onto the Banbury Road, headed north to Wolvercote. They passed through the village and crossed the river by the Trout Pub and pulled into a field. In front of them were the ruins of Godstow Nunnery.

It took about thirty minutes to set up the various crates, the so-called quaser, the projector (those were the bits James managed to recognise). The quaser resembled a modest sized search light. It was placed on a tripod about three metres from the building. There were also some funny-looking foot-square cubes that he had been told were mainly made of glass and very fragile, plus some flight cases containing computer-type devices. The other bloke, who was introduced as Steve, set up a mini-generator that chugged away, breaking the silence of the late summer countryside idyll.

The three scientists spoke to each other about the setup, including James in the conversation.

'We won't get that wide an angle,' said Steve. 'Let's concentrate on a doorway or section of wall, a window or something this time.'

'What about this ground floor window here?' said Mongoose.

They were standing outside the ruin which was really just a very large sandstone outer shell with no roof or much internal structure. Grass grew within.

Near the van they set up a normal projection screen. 'We can do it in 3D, but it means carrying a load more stuff. So we'll just have this screen to look at,' said Mel.

The sun had dropped into the hazy clouds on the horizon and, at 7pm, the daylight was starting to fade.

'I think we're ready,' said Steve.

A number of switches were switched by all three, buttons

pressed and codes typed in on a PC keyboard.

Then, a curious thing happened.

As the quaser came on, the beam that presumably came out of it was like nothing James could have expected. Where once had been a wall of eroded stone and a single window with a bit of the original frame, he now saw nothing. The section of wall, about three metres across and three metres high, was in total darkness, whereas the rest of the wall wasn't. It was as if the searchlight was shining a beam of black light, or as if it was sucking the light right out of the wall.

James was the only one looking at the wall. The others had their eyes on the projection screen which was now illuminated with a projection of the wall and window, just as it had looked moments earlier.

'OK, this is the present,' said Mel. 'Let's take it back, Goose.'

Mongoose entered something on his keyboard.

'What have we got?' said Mel. The image looked the same.

'About 1950. I'm going back in units of 64 years again, like before. It's easier,' Goose said.

Then the projection changed. The stone was less eroded, and the window frame was complete, but no glass.

'1640s,' said Goose.

'Still a ruin then. Let's go back further to where we went before,' said Steve.

'1170,' said Goose.

Then everyone froze. The window was now completely 'restored', with glass and leading. Looking through the window was a young woman, her face pressed up to the glass, shouting. Of course, there was no sound, but none of the four would have needed to be a lip-reading expert to know what she was shouting. The girl seemed to be looking directly at them, her desperate eyes staring out from the projection screen, screaming in silence with what looked like 'Go away!'

Mel turned off the machines. The screen faded to black, and the wall faded into daylight. 'It worked. Better than before, I think,' she said.

James stood there, quite pale. 'That girl...' he said.

'Congratulations,' said Goose. 'You've seen your first proper ghost.'

He'd calmed down by the time they'd packed away the equipment and it had started to get a bit dark.

'So we were looking into the past? She couldn't see us?' said James.

'She looked out of that window sometime in 1170, and we dialled back the quaser and saw what we'd have seen had we stood here back then. But of course, she couldn't see us. It was just a projection,' said Mel as they climbed back into the van.

'I wonder what happened?' said James.

'She probably fell foul of the nuns and got locked up in that room for not being chaste or something,' said Steve.

'Was it the same girl as before?' said Goose.

'Yes, I think so,' said Mel.

'You've been here before?' asked James.

'Yes. Last time we set up inside the ruin, but the beam wasn't powerful enough to light up much. But we did get a strong image of a girl, probably that girl, standing still in what appeared to be a hall inside,' said Mel. 'That's when we discovered an interesting side effect, and we worked out why didn't see much inside. For some reason, we don't quite know yet, we can only look into the past along light that hasn't been viewed by the human eye. We don't know why.'

'So we can only view scenes that no-one else has seen,' added Goose. 'If we do, the screen has dark patches. It's weird, like a feedback loop. If it's been seen by someone, we can't see it.'

'Where are we going now?' said James.

'We'll drop the stuff off at the lab and then go for a drink at the Eagle and Child, eh?' said Goose.

'No, wait. I've got an idea. Can we go to my house? St Mary's Road in Cowley. We had a break-in last night. If we set up the machine there, we might just be able to see who did it. What do you think?'

'I'm game,' said Steve.

'Real detective work,' said Goose.

'Ok, let's try it,' said Mel.

By nine o'clock, they'd set up once again in the cramped front room of the terrace house. It was Jane's room, chosen because it was the tidiest to accommodate all the gear, and her laptop had been stolen from the desk in the bay window, so they'd have a real good focus to aim the quaser.

Jane wasn't in, fortunately, thought James. His desire to catch the villain outweighed the feeling that marching into someone's room was another invasion of privacy, and he felt that Jane would be better off not knowing until they had something to report. She'd been so upset by the break-in earlier. He set up his video camera pointing at the projection screen to capture what they might find.

The process at the ruin was repeated, the black light beamed out, and the entire bay window was hidden in blackness. The projection screen lit up to show a desk with a laptop on it.

'Sorry, gone back too far already. What time do we think the burglar was here?' said Goose.

'Don't know exactly. Between eight and ten, we think,' said James.

On the screen, Jane appeared, sitting at the desk which they could now no longer see. Whatever Jane looked at in the scene was blacked out. She got up and walked out of the scene, and the desk returned. The laptop was still there.

'Bring it forward a bit more,' said Mel.

Then, a short scrawny man appeared in the room, his head covered with a hoodie and a heavy bag over one shoulder. As he

looked around the room, those areas of it were bathed in blackness.
'Come on,' said James under his breath. 'Let's see your face...'
Then the man turned to face the door on the left and just as they got
to get a glimpse of his face, the screen went black.

'What's happened?' asked James.

'Someone must have come into the room and seen him, so
now we can't see it as it's already been viewed,' said Mel.

'Who would that be? I thought no-one was at home?'
said Steve.

'No, Jane was still in,' replied James.

Then the image came back. They all saw the man, with a knife
in hand, holding it above what looked like someone he was holding
down on the floor. It looked like he was about to strike the figure
with it, but then he looked up instead, and stared right at them. In
his eyes was the look of fear. He seemed to back off, released the
figure on the floor, and ran out of the room.

'I think we've got him,' said James. 'Can we pack up quick
before Jane gets back?'

'She not only saw him, he attacked her,' said Mel. 'Why didn't
she mention that before?'

'She was pretty much in shock when I came back last night.
Now we know why,' James said.

It was late and there wasn't time to go to the pub that night so
James stayed and the other three returned in their van back to the
laboratory. He went to his room upstairs. Something was bothering

him. Jane had been saved by something frightening the intruder. Thinking back to the Godstow experiment, the girl in 1170 had the same look in her eye. They both appeared to look directly at them as they viewed the screen. That meant they had appeared to look directly at the location of the quaser. But that was, of course, impossible as the quaser wasn't there when those past events took place. As Mel had said, they were just viewing the past, like a recording. And amazing though that was, that's all it was.

Annoyed to remember that his computer was gone, James took out his phone and did a search for information on Godstow Abbey. It was famous as the final burial place of the famed beauty Rosamund Clifford, known as Fair Rosamund, who had been a long-term mistress of Henry II. Henry's liaison with Rosamund became public knowledge in 1174, and she had gone into hiding in the nunnery at Godstow in 1176, shortly before her death.

Interesting though that was, none of that helped, it seemed. Then James clicked a link in the reference on the website to a site about haunted Oxfordshire. There he found a short article about the ghost of a young girl, thought to be a nun, at Godstow. There had been numerous sightings of her through the centuries 'always running away from something'. One report claimed to give a backstory for the ghost and cited the execution of a nun in 1170 who the Church had feared was a witch. Her trial had been based on reports that she'd claimed to have repeatedly seen three, or sometimes four, 'demons' appearing in and around the abbey, staring at her.

James paused for a moment, and then read the next and final part, which caused a chill to run up his spine. The convicted girl described the evil spirits as appearing in human form, one of them 'being a maiden having a pink stripe running through her hair.'

Unexpected
Signature of Life

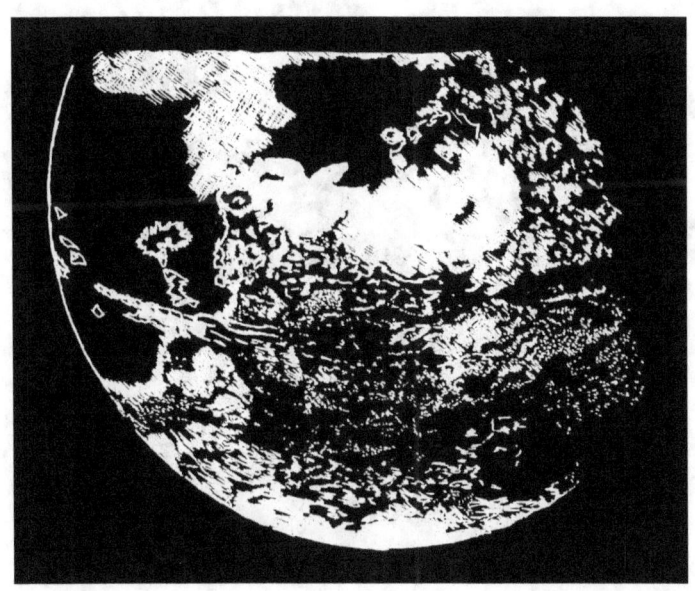

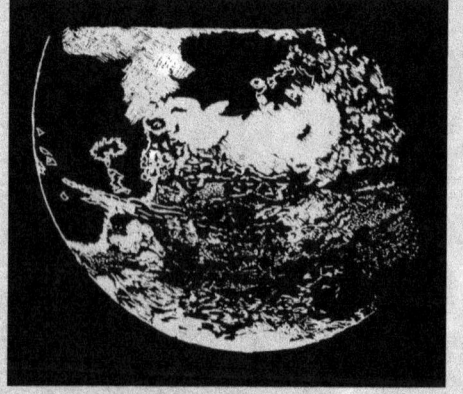

Unexpected
Signature of Life

The Viking and Pathfinder probes showed a rock-strewn and dusty landscape on Mars with no obvious signs of life. Nothing unexpected there.

'It's too cold for life,' the scientists said. 'The average temperature is minus sixty three degrees Celsius. Also, there's just not enough water. There can be no life on Mars. Maybe two billion years ago there may have been rivers. Maybe back then there could have been life. There's evidence of subsurface water drainage, water-ice erosion and geological structures consistent with ancient shorelines, gorges and islands. But the atmospheric pressure is too low. Any water below forty degrees of latitude sublimes directly into gas. Life also requires oxygen. The atmosphere is mainly carbon dioxide.'

The scientists did not believe that life was possible on Mars.

'Perhaps billions of years ago there could have been simple bacteria-type life forms. Meteorite ALH84001, if it did come from Mars, could contain what may be ancient Martian micro fossils.' The scientists did not believe that there could possibly be advanced forms of life, maybe even intelligent life, still living on Mars today.

'Certainly not,' the scientists said. 'How could there be? The planet is utterly inhospitable. Haven't you been listening? Didn't you pay any attention at college? We've looked for living bacteria with the Gas Exchange Experiments. We've added Martian soil to nineteen amino acids, looking for hydrogen, nitrogen, oxygen, carbon dioxide and methane given off by any living organisms. The results were 'false positive'; they produced the gases too much, too fast and also at too high temperatures. There were no biological reactions.'

Maybe not. But what were the scientists looking for? What is life's real signature?

The year is 2036 by their chronological method. The first humans are about to step onto another world. They have travelled hundreds of millions of miles through space on a journey that has taken six individuals two years, but taken humanity fifteen billion years. 'Humanity' is the name given to most recently evolved form of mobile body used to carry the replicating genes locked into the highly successful DNA molecule. DNA has, in recent aeons, become the only form of life on the third planet. So much so, that the various intelligences that it has helped to form believe that it is the only form that life can take.

They didn't expect anything to surprise them. Rocks, dust, dry ice, more rocks, pink sky.

'Mars will be a quiet and peaceful place,' the scientists said.

They had taken photographs, spectrographs and chromatographs. They knew exactly what they would see when they stepped out onto the surface of Mars. But no-one had ever taken an audio recording of the planet. No-one had ever listened to Mars.

When the first humans landed, they were deafened by the sound. The sound of life. The scientists had looked for the physical evidence of chemical reactions, of amino acids, proteins, RNA and DNA replicators, and other biological signatures. But they were totally unprepared for an assault on their auditory senses.

The life on Mars had, like the life on Earth, evolved from random fluctuations, not in chemical molecular reactions, but in physical interaction and electrostatic transitions creating a deafening cacophony of living vibrations within the human range of hearing.

But the vibrations didn't stop at deafening the humans. The electronic vibrations shook their DNA apart, breaking it down, consuming it, giving off hydrogen, nitrogen, oxygen, carbon dioxide and methane as it did so.

The scientists were right. There were no biological organisms on Mars, and after the human Mars mission in 2036 there continued to be none.

But Mars was seething with life.

Danger! Dragons have been Sighted Recently in this Vicinity

Danger! Dragons have been Sighted Recently in this Vicinity

In the days when the land had many kingdoms, there once was a small and peaceful village. Peaceful, that was, in the days before the dragon came.

The people who lived there were very happy, even though they didn't have very much, but then there was nothing really that they could have wanted. That was, until the dragon came.

Bill the miller was a calm and friendly fellow. That is, until he met the dragon. No-one had a bad word to say against Bill, but then no-one had a bad word to say against anyone. But sadly that all changed when the dragon came.

Pat was on his way up the hill to the mill. It was a hot sunny day. A wonderful day, Pat thought to himself. But then, it was always a wonderful day. Pat had yet to meet the dragon.

Pat came up to the mill house. He called for Bill, but he wasn't there. He knocked on the door, but there was no answer. He opened the door and went in. Bill was inside, sitting at a table with his back to the door.

'Hello Bill,' said Pat.

'Do you mind?' said Bill.

'Mind what?' asked Pat.

'Barging in to people's homes when they're busy,' Bill spat.

'But it's only me,' said Pat, surprised. 'I've come for some flour.'

'Well, you can't have any,' said Bill, finally turning round.

'Why not?' asked Pat, puzzled. 'Is something wrong?'

'Nothing is wrong. Now, I'm a busy man, so good-day,' said Bill. He turned back to the table and continued using the scales.

Pat scratched his head, trying to make sense of the situation.

'Are you ill?' he said at last.

'No I am not,' retorted Bill.

'There are sacks of flour outside. You surely can't mean to keep them all for yourself? What will you do with them all?' said Pat.

'Those sacks have been sold to some merchants in the Town in the Valley, and there is none left for you.'

'Well, will there be any more tomorrow? We've had a good harvest this year, and no mistake. There'll be more than enough for the Town in the Valley and us…' Pat was cut off mid-sentence.

'There will be no spare flour tomorrow or the next day or the day after that. I have a contract signed for this harvest and the next, so good-day.' Bill was beginning to lose patience.

'But I'm the baker for the whole village. What will I bake

with?' said Pat, a little upset.

'That's up to you,' replied Bill.

'But what will the village eat?' said Pat, with tears in his eyes.

'Let them eat turnips,' was Bill's response.

Pat left the mill and wiped his tears. He was now quite angry.

In the morning, Bill noticed that two of his sacks of flour were missing from outside the mill. Cursing the baker's name, he set off into town.

Jon the Innkeeper was a very jolly fellow indeed, and was well known for it, too. It was mid-morning when he arrived at the bakery, a smile on his face as he smelt the delicious smell of freshly baked bread.

'Good-day to you, Pat,' he called out as he approached the bakery door.

'What's good about it?' was the response from inside.

'Is that you, Pat?' said Jon, puzzled.

'What do you want? I'm very busy,' said Pat as he appeared at the bakery door.

'Well, my old friend, I'd like a dozen buns and three of your finest fresh loaves, if you please,' said Jon.

Pat disappeared into the bakery and emerged a minute later with only half a dozen buns and two stale loaves. Jon exchanged the bread for a small purse of coins.

As soon as it was in his hands, Pat tipped the contents of the purse into his palm. 'I'm afraid that's not enough,' said Pat.

'But that's the usual amount,' said Jon.

'Well the usual amount isn't good enough anymore,' said Pat.

'Why ever not? We had a wonderful harvest this year, and no mistake…' Jon said before being cut off mid-sentence.

'I have to earn a living, you know. Do you realise I have to ride all the way into the Town in the Valley to get my flour now, and at almost twice the cost?' said Pat angrily.

Jon's jolly smile was now gone. 'Well, seeing that I'm an honest man, here's your money.' He counted out some extra coins into Pat's hand. 'And I'll bid you as good a day as you deserve.' With that, he left.

When Jon arrived home, he noticed that he was a loaf short and that the bread was stale. He cursed the baker as he got the barrels of ale ready for lunchtime.

The first customer at the Tavern that day was Tom the blacksmith. Tom was the first customer to arrive at the Tavern every lunchtime. No-one minded however. It was said that he was the hardest worker in the entire village. He had recently finished shoeing the entire garrison for the Prince, which must have been well over three score of horses.

Tom didn't need to be asked what he wanted to drink that day; neither did he need to ask. Even the term 'my usual' was redundant since what was usual was what he wanted everyday anyhow, and that was two pints of 'Mottled Bog Grobble', the local brew. So Tom was very surprised to find that his two pints weren't waiting for him at noon on the bench outside. Something must be wrong, he thought, so he went inside.

Behind the bar he found Jon, arranging some stale buns.

'Afternoon' said Tom.

'Oh, hello Tom,' replied Jon, not looking up.

'What seems to be the matter?' enquired Tom.

'It just doesn't seem to be a very good day,' replied Jon.

'But it's always a good day. Maybe the summer's nearly over, but that's no reason to feel that it's not a good day, by any means,' said Tom.

'Although it pains me, and don't get me wrong, I've thought long and hard about this,' said Jon. 'I've decided to put up the price of my ale. The cost of my living is certainly not what it used to be, and I'm not running a charity here, you know. You do understand what I mean, don't you?'

'I can't say I'm pleased about it, especially as that'll mean that I'll have to get by on only one pint of ale for my lunch,' replied Tom.

'What do you mean?' said Jon raising his voice slightly. 'You're rolling in it. Especially after all the Prince's horses. I dare say he paid you extra for such an important job.'

'Well, it's no lie that he didn't offer more than the job was worth, but I like to think of myself as an honest man, and I charged him the going rate that I would have charged anyone,' Tom replied calmly.

By this time Jon had poured Tom his pint. Tom reluctantly handed over the new, higher amount.

'Now I've been meaning to ask you,' said Jon, who'd calmed down now. 'I want my horse shod. I've been putting it off for weeks, but now it really needs to be done.'

'I can fit you in next week,' said Tom.

'Next week?' snapped Jon. 'I need it done now. This afternoon, if you don't mind.'

Tom tried to remain calm. 'I'm afraid this afternoon's not my own to give. I have six jobs to do today, and the palace gate to start tomorrow. If you'd come to me earlier, I might have been able to fit you in but...'

Jon cut him off mid-sentence. 'I can see that you're all high and mighty now that you're in with the Prince. What with the blacksmith's craft being such a simple one, I'm surprised you can't do all those jobs in an hour. Unless, of course, you find horses too difficult now that the easy option of a plain gate has come up.'

'I'd have you know that my craft takes years of apprenticing to fully learn all the skills. What's more, the gate I have designed for the palace will rank among the finest in the land,' Tom replied angrily. 'Then perhaps you are just plain lazy, and expensive, too,' said Jon. 'I'd wager I'll find a more reasonable blacksmith in the Town in the Valley.'

'Then you do that!' shouted Tom who gulped down the

remainder of his pint and walked angrily out of the Tavern.

Tom got back to the smithy to find that his furnace had gone down. He cursed the innkeeper for delaying him so that he hadn't come back in time to put more wood on the fire. He went round to his wood shed only to find that he was seriously low on wood. Well, since the fire was going out, no more work could really be done today. He didn't really feel like working anyway, so he set off for the woodcutter's cottage to get a cart load of logs.

Now it was said that the woodcutter's daughter was the most beautiful maiden in the whole village, and that no man short of the Prince would be worthy of such beauty. In fact, unbeknownst to her and her father, the Prince, while visiting the village, had indeed noticed her.

She saw the blacksmith coming down the track from the window of the cottage and went outside to meet him.

She explained that her father had gone into the Town in the Valley to arrange for the sale of their cottage, as he had been talking to the miller about the opportunities in the Town, and that woodcutting was a dying trade and business had been falling.

'So what am I to do?' said Tom.

'You'll have to sort that out for yourself,' responded the woodcutter's daughter.

'What are you talking about? Have you gone mad?' snapped

Tom. 'I'm the most important blacksmith in the land, if not the entire kingdom. I haven't got time for this nonsense.' And with that, he left.

'What a rude fellow,' said the woodcutter's daughter to herself as she went back inside the cottage to continue packing her things.

It wasn't very long before the woodcutter and his daughter left the village and started a new life in the Town in the Valley. The woodcutter became a builder, with a good wage. He worked very hard and built some of the finest walls in the Town, but he was just one builder among many.

The blacksmith soon moved to the Prince's court where he continued to do fine work, but only the Prince saw it, and since he had come to expect it, he didn't really pay much attention anymore. The miller spent all the time he wasn't making flour travelling back and forward to the Town in the Valley. He couldn't move there as there were no fields or room for a mill.

Both the baker and the innkeeper moved to the Town in the Valley, too. Both tried to do better than they did before, but both ended up much worse.

It was a year to the day since Pat had first walked up the hill to find Bill the miller in a foul mood when the Prince returned to the small village. He rode past the bakery, with its boarded up windows. He rode past the inn, which was closed. He rode past the old smithy in which someone was now keeping chickens, and he rode down the track to the woodcutter's cottage.

'There doesn't appear to be anyone living here, sire,' said the Prince's kinsman. 'Are you sure she was here?'

'Her beauty does now seem like it could have only been a dream, and yet I know that I met her, here in these woods,' said the Prince. 'But you are right. There is no-one here now. Let us return to the village and see what word we can find there.'

'A word we may find only when we come across a living soul to utter it, sire, and no living soul have we sighted since we left the palace.' said the kinsman as they turned their horses around and galloped off to the centre of the village once more.

They rode up to the mill, only to find an impregnable wall which the miller had a builder from the Town in the Valley build for him to keep out thieves. The Prince and his kinsman found no-one to talk to there. They were about to leave the village altogether when they spotted an old man with a long grey beard, walking out of the village very slowly, leaning on a stick. The two men rode up to him.

'Old man, this is your Prince. Prey tell us what has become of the village?' said the Prince.

The old man looked up slowly. 'You mean to say that you don't know?'

'Know what?' asked the kinsman. 'Speak up, man.'

The old man addressed the kinsman. 'It is said that your master is amongst the most noble, honest and righteous of men that ever should have lived. Is this true?'

'Of course,' said the kinsman. 'Does any man question the character of my master?'

'Not I, for I know not,' said the old man, 'But I will tell you this much. If what you say is true, and you both be honourable in your thoughts, words, and deeds, then promise me you will do my bidding by heeding my advice.'

'What rot is this?' said the kinsman. 'Shall I have this impertinent weasel's throat cut, for such an offer must surely hide devious intent.'

'Let the old man give us his advice,' replied the Prince. 'We shall use our reasoning to judge if his words are fair.' He turned to the old man. 'Tell us what is in your heart, old man.'

The old man breathed deeply, maybe because of the gravity of the words he was about to impart, or perhaps just for effect.

'A year ago,' he said, 'the dragon came to the village. I would warn you. Do not ever enter the Town in the Valley, for that is his domain, and the people there his subjects. Put out a warning to the far reaching corners of your kingdom that the dragon has been here.'

The Prince thanked the old man and indeed did not return to the village as long as he did live. He did, however, visit the Town in the Valley, but he rode right past the beautiful woodcutter's daughter as she was just one beautiful maiden among many.

I Saw
Faeries One
Christmas Eve

I Saw
Faeries One
Christmas Eve

When I was younger, I saw faeries. I don't expect you to believe me because you don't know what faeries are. But they were real.

They were dressed in gold, or glittered and glowed like gold, as they flew overhead, way above the trees. A few at first, and then a lot more circled back. They carried long thin trumpets which they blew, but I heard no sound. I imagined I heard a sound like tinkling glass. It was a procession, like a faerie float. Along came glowing carriages, delicate chariots pulled by the winged creatures. There was a sense of celebration, of joy. I knew they were announcing the arrival of Christmas. It was Christmas Eve. I was four years old.

I never saw them again, but I did see some of their kin a couple of years later. I awoke in a cold sweat, after having a frightening feeling of falling. My bad dreams were over, and I was back in my bed, on the top bunk, safe. I wasn't dead or trapped in an upside-down inside-out dimension of shadows where no-one could hear my cries. I hadn't been left upside down on the dark side of the Moon. The world of my bedroom was normal and sensible and the right way up again.

'The world isn't normal and sensible,' said a voice.

I froze. Where did that voice come from? Was it inside my head? It seemed to have come from outside though, from the figure that stood by the door. A dark humanoid shape, like a hooded figure, hanging there.

'You're frightened,' said the shadow. 'Frightened of me.'

'No I'm not,' I said.

'Don't lie,' the figure snapped. 'I know what you know.'

'You're just my dressing gown hung on the back of the door,' I said, not really believing it was that simple.

'Then why are you talking to me?' said the voice.

'I'm making this all up. You don't exist. You're in my head.'

'Then you are quite mad.'

'All right, so I am frightened. That's nothing to be ashamed of. You are just a dressing gown though. Hung on a hook. I'll unhook you, and you'll fall to the floor,' I said bravely.

'You are too frightened to move. I am Spook. I am the spirit that lives in the shape of your dressing gown. And we are not alone, as you can see.'

I looked around the room. Within the plastic light-shade, a myriad of delicate glowing faerie creatures flittered back and forth, whispering in high pitched singsong voices. Then I was aware of something else. Under my pillow was a kingdom of tiny two-dimensional people going about their business.

'What is all this?' I asked. 'What's happening?'

'Nothing is happening that doesn't always happen,' said the voice of Spook. 'Now your mind is open to the possibilities that do exist. Now your perception isn't filtering them all out. Now you are a part of the realm, and it is a part of you.'

'This reminds me of more things,' I said, or thought (the two are the same). 'Dreams that I had. I walked out into the garden; the sky was full of stars, all moving about. In the centre of the garden was a tree with copper leaves, like milk bottle tops. There was music in the wind, and the place was lit like day, but it was the middle of the night.'

'Dreams are but the greater reality between the dreams of reality,' said Spook.

'I don't understand,' I said.

'You will. Look out of the window.'

I climbed down off the bed and looked outside and there they were. The sky was full of stars and other lights. They looked like odd little helicopters, but they made no sound. They moved as though they were dancing, living lights, all different shapes and sizes, all different distances in the sky and in space.

'What are they doing?' I asked.

'Getting ready for what you call Christmas,' the voice replied.

I crept to the door and unhooked the label of the dressing gown from the hook. It fell to the floor. The faeries in the light-shade flittered out through the window, and the kingdom under the pillow slipped into tranquility, despite the head that was now tucked underneath it and the quilt.

I never saw those creatures again. But every night, I'd gaze out of the window, hoping for one more glimpse. Even as an adult, I quietly creep outside into the garden, alone, close to midnight on Christmas Eve, and look up into the grey night. I hope beyond hope that my eyes haven't grown too old to see.

But I never hung my dressing gown on the back of the door again.

The Magic Candle

The
Magic Candle

I stared out of my bedroom window onto the road below. The snow had started falling quite heavily. The wind had picked up again and was blowing the snow into small drifts up the pavement curb. I desperately wanted to go out and play, but my mum wouldn't let me because I had some homework to do. I turned to look back into my drab room. There on the table lay my exercise book and pencil case. Mrs. Reed had asked me to write a story. An impossible task.

'Couldn't I draw a comic strip?' I had asked. I was seven.

'Certainly not,' she had replied. 'I want you to write a story using words, not pictures, and I want you to come up with something original.' She had spoken to the whole class, but she really meant it for just me. 'That means I don't want to be reading about spaceships and monsters from your favourite television programmes,' she said. She was referring to *Doctor Who*.

So what was I to do? I looked out at the snow. There was no sign of the curb now. It was if it had never been there. I wanted to jump from the pavement into the deep snow which covered the road. But I couldn't. I had to stay in my room and write a boring story instead. First though, I would look at the snow, falling past the street lamp. Each snowflake seemed alive. They were like a swarm of bees, dark against the sky. Trying to follow an individual one on its journey from the sky to the ground was mesmerising. I sat there by the windowsill, holding onto my talking Dalek, positioned so he could see out, too.

I was suddenly aware that night had fallen. So gradual had dusk been that I hadn't noticed until I found that my room was in darkness. The gentle falling snow had now given way to a blizzard. I stumbled back into my room to turn the light on, but it didn't work. I walked out onto the landing. It was also in darkness. Could it be a power cut? Great, I wouldn't have to write the story.

Mum shouted up from downstairs. I could see that she was positioning candles in the hall. 'Do you want one up there?' she shouted up.

'No thanks, I've got my torch,' I replied in dismay and went back into my room to get it.

My torch consisted of a bulb, a battery and a switch connected together in a small box. I had made it. I flicked the switch. The bulb glowed dimly. The battery was flat. So a candle was needed after all, and I went downstairs to find one.

I tiptoed through the candlelit hall and stepped into the dark unlit kitchen. I made my way clumsily to the sink and fumbled in a cupboard underneath it, eventually pulling out an old wooden box. In it I could make out a metal candlestick holder which appeared to hold the only candle left, and a small box of matches. Clutching my newly found treasures, I returned to my room. Once inside, I closed the door and set the candle on my table and lit it.

The room looked different by candlelight. Nothing seemed to have any solid, stable form. The flickering yellow light threw dark, sharp shadows that made the room feel a lot bigger. The room seemed quieter too. The only sound was of the wind, occasionally blowing the snow against my window.

I looked over my shoulder, convinced that someone was there. Nobody was. I opened my exercise book and picked up my pencil. Now, what should I write about? I looked again at the flickering flame and once more had the feeling that someone, or something was watching me. But there was only darkness. I began to write: There was a power cut on a wintry night, and I lit a magic candle. Things began to change.

At this, I was quite pleased with myself, and drew a little picture of the short stubby candle in its old fashioned brass holder. It was just like the one Wee Willie Winkie had, I thought, and added some more detail to the picture. I looked at the flame to try and draw a good likeness, but it was so bright that it gave a purple after image on my eyes, so I couldn't see clearly enough to draw.

The wind began to howl, and I shivered. It was suddenly very cold in the room. I held my cold fingers close to the flame for warmth. Then came that strange feeling again. I picked up the candle holder. A gust of icy wind blew into my face. I turned around and looked out over fields and fields of snow. The snow had stopped falling, and the sky was clear allowing a full moon to shine down on the blanket of soft snow, lighting it up a sparkling white. I looked down at my feet. The table had gone; the room had gone; my house had gone; my entire street had gone. Turning around, I could see the village church in the distance, with a cluster of buildings around it. The church seemed to be the same distance away from my house as it always had been. I then felt an extra shiver, on top of the one due to the cold—as if I had somehow travelled in time and now stood in the field in which my house had yet to be built.

From some distance away, I could see what appeared to be a mound of snow moving towards me. As it got nearer, I could see that it was a large white animal, a polar bear. I was too cold to know what to do, whether to run or not, so I just stood there, teeth chattering, frozen in fear.

'You are cold,' said the polar bear.

'Yes,' I replied, too cold to care that a polar bear had just spoken to me.

'Follow me,' said the bear. I did as I was told.

We waded through the snow to the edge of a wood. I immediately felt warmer.

'What's in here?' I asked the bear.

'You'll see,' said the bear as we continued to walk into the wood. The snow became thinner as we went deeper in. I became aware of strange scents, like cinnamon and spices. I could almost hear lilting music.

Eventually we entered a large clearing. I could now see the

source of the strange music and sweet smells. It was some sort of fair, but like no fair I had ever seen before. People were dancing and singing. There were stalls which were serving food. All around was a kaleidoscope of colour. The music was coming from a group of musicians and a pipe organ which was next to a huge carousel with hobbyhorses going round and round.

I stepped into the clearing and looked around to see what the polar bear was going to do next, but it had gone. Then, a man who had been attending a large pile of logs and twigs approached me.

'Ah, there you are,' said the man. He was decidedly odd, dressed in a green tunic. He had sharp pointed features and wasn't much taller than me. I looked around, not believing it was me who the little man was talking to. Everybody else carried on doing their own thing. They, too, looked more than a little odd, now I had properly noticed them.

Come this way,' said the little man, and walked off in the direction of the pile of logs and twigs. All the other little people then began to make their way to circle around me, the little man and the log pile.

Well?' said the little man.

'What?' I asked, a little nervous because everybody was looking at me. The man pointed to my right hand. I looked down, and to my surprise I was still carrying the candle. What was more, it was still alight. The man then pointed to the twigs. Did they want me to light their fire? I knelt down and touched the candle's flame to the dry leaves at the base of the pile. The fire soon took hold. The people cheered and resumed their merriment.

'What do I do now?' I asked, as the man turned to join the throng.

'Have you got enough for a story now?' said the man.

'Oh,' I said. "I suppose so.'

'Then you had better get writing,' said the man, starting to walk off into the crowd.

'But how can I get back?' I shouted after him in despair.

'Blow out the candle,' came the reply.

Well, that's easy enough, I thought. But before I go, I'll have a go on that merry-go-round. I made my way over to it. Another little man stopped the carousel, and I climbed onto a black steed. I looked down at all the little people dancing round the fire as the merry-go-round took up speed, but as it did so, the candle blew out, and I found myself suddenly still, in the dark silence once more.

I was back in my room, crouched on top of the table. I climbed down and tried the light switch. This time it worked. The light came on, and the room was back to its usual, dreary, normal appearance.

I put the candle down and sat at the table. Picking up my pencil, I began to write. I wrote and wrote and wrote, until the entire tale had been told from the magic candle to the polar bear to the merry-go-round and back to the magic candle.

Then at last it was finished, and I put my pencil down.

There was a knock on the door. It was my mum.

'The news forecast says that all the roads are blocked, and the village is cut off. So it looks like there won't be any school tomorrow. That'll give you an extra day to write your story.'

I went over to the window and looked out onto the featureless white landscape.

'Well, now I've finished the story, I can have a whole day playing in the snow!'

And, do you know? I did.

Stars

Stars

It was a pleasantly cool night. The boy looked away from the fire and threw his head back to gaze at the stars. It was a while before the after-image from the fire faded. Then he could see them: hundreds and thousands of tiny points of light.

'Tell me about the stars, father,' he asked. His father was spooning more broth into his wooden bowl.

'The stars are the stars, and that is all,' replied his father.

'Yes but,' the boy continued, "why are they there? What are they for?'

'Haven't I told you before?' his father said unemotionally as he sipped his soup. 'The stars are of heaven, and of heaven we must not concern ourselves. The earth is our home; the soils and the seas are our living. Heaven is for the dead.'

'But I only want to know,' the boy said frustratedly.

'It is not for us to know. It's unlucky to dwell on such things.'

Later that night, the boy was lying in his bed. He wished he could sleep outside, under the stars. Maybe then they would give up their secrets. He began to grow fearful. The light from his candle threw flickering amber shadows on the wall in eerie human shapes, twisted and contorted, as if alive and angry. Perhaps his father was right.

Then his mother entered to wish him good-night. The light from her candle sent the shadow men running for cover in the dark corners of the room.

'Mother, don't go just yet. Tell me a story.'

She sat down on the side of the bed. 'What did you do to anger your father this evening?' she asked.

'I asked him about the stars, that was all,' the boy replied.

'Well, let me tell you the story of Icranos the Fool and his mighty Ship,' she said soothingly. 'A long time ago, there were many more people in the world. They didn't live with their families in shelters like we do today, but in mighty castles in an even larger castle called the City. They lived in a time of abundance and joy. There was so much food that no-one went hungry. There were no diseases, and people lived much longer than they do now, to nearly a hundred years. They were masters of everything on earth, and only one more thing was left unknown to them. Do you know what that was?'

'Was it the stars?' said the boy.

'Yes, the stars. Icranos worked out a way to sail into heaven. He designed an enormous Ship that he thought would be able to sail up to and past the stars, to the edge of the universe. But to build such a Ship, he would need everybody's help, and all the iron and steel and copper of the world.'

The boy interrupted her, 'A ship made of steel? Like your ring?'

'Yes exactly like it, but remember: metals were not as rare as they are today.'

The boy was deep in thought, trying to imagine something so huge made from something so precious. His mother continued.

'After ten years of work, the Ship was nowhere near finished. The people said they were fed up with building it, and that it would never work. Icranos grew angry and overthrew the leaders of the people and enslaved everyone to work for him. After another twenty years, the Ship was finished, but at a great cost.

'As the Ship set sail for heaven, all the mighty castles were smashed to the ground, and a ferocious fiery wind swept through the City, killing everyone in its path. Those that survived found Icranos and his Ship gone. But worse was that heaven had sent a great plague in return for Icranos's folly. Many more people died, and their crops failed year after year. And now we have many diseases, and life is much harder, as a reminder of that fateful day.'

'So what happened to the Ship? Where did Icranos go?' asked the boy.

'Some say he perished, along with the Ship in the fire. Others say he did, indeed, ascend to heaven and set off for the edge of the universe.'

In the morning, the boy asked his father about Icranos and the Ship. His father snapped his reply in his usual dismissive fashion.
'What rubbish has your mother been telling you? They're just fairy stories made up by fools to try to make sense of life.'

'But father,' the boy protested, 'they lived in a City like a mighty castle. Maybe the Plateau of Tombs was part of it.'

'Those ruins?' responded the father. 'They're thousands of years old, the burial places for the dead. The ancients didn't bury their dead in the soil as we do, but in those enormous strange stone boxes.'

'But father,' the boy continued, 'maybe they didn't bury people there. Maybe they lived there. Maybe the Tombs were part of the City.'

'I've had just about enough of this nonsense. I don't want to hear another word about it, and I'll have a word with your mother, too. These fairy stories are corrupting your young mind.'

Long Night of the Dragon

Long Night
of the Dragon

Darrel was excited. He rushed into Professor Warrad's office. Warrad didn't look up.

'What are you still doing here?' the old professor asked him. 'I would have thought that a young man like you would have been preparing himself for the celebrations.'

'Later, maybe,' Darrel responded hurriedly. 'Professor, I've been working on a theory…'

Warrad interrupted him politely. 'Mr Yarm, I am aware of your good work. Your thesis on gravitation was received very well indeed by everyone in the scientific community.'

Darrel dismissed him. 'I don't mean that. I've been working on something else. Something quite different, and I have to tell you. To find out what you think. Tonight.'

'Tonight?'

'Yes, tonight. You see, it's about tonight, the 'Long Night of the Dragon'. I won't be able to relax, never mind celebrate, until I've discussed my findings with someone. Someone who'd be able to understand, of course.'

'Then sit down, Mr Yarm.' the professor said calmly. 'What do you want to tell me?'

Darrel placed a file down on the professor's untidy desk. 'It began when I was reading an old copy of the Scriptures at my parents' house. It had been my grandmother's copy, which was printed before the Reformation which brought in the current translation. As I had been brought up with the new version, I was surprised how different it seemed to what I remembered.'

'Different? In what way?' said the professor.

'I'm not just talking about the old language and grammar. I mean facts. Most notably concerning the 'Long Night of the Dragon'. The main section is the part when the Dragon first appears. Both versions have the prophet Harron saying, 'A new star appeared in the sky'. Now, in the new translation, Harron then goes on to describe the star getting closer until he could see the shape of the dragon: 'the shape shone in the sun, and I could see that it was a dragon, flying towards me out of the blue sky.' Notice that he already refers to it as a dragon, and that it appears as such in the daytime. If it was day time, why did he describe it as a star if stars are only visible at night?'

'Perhaps it was bright enough in the light of the sun to shine like a star during the day,' said the professor. 'Or more likely, whatever it really was, it was burning up on entering the atmosphere.'

'Right, but listen to what the old translation says. There is a whole extra paragraph describing the object as a new star, passing by overhead a number of times during the night, before Harron sees it again during the day when it is a lot closer. It sounds like he's describing something that was in a decaying orbit,' said the professor. 'Typical of the priest to edit that part out to make the object seem more like a dragon than a meteorite.'

'That's what I thought. Listen to this part,' continued Darrel. 'The next section describes the 'dragon' passing over the cities in both countries, and says that it caused so much fear that a war that had been raging for a thousand years ended.'

'The dragon taught us that we had a greater enemy than each other, and that only together could we frighten it away, or some such nonsense,' the professor said.

'What it says is that the dragon had 'its mouth wide open, its wings beside its body, and fire streaming from its nose'. It goes on to describe how it plunged the land into darkness for a night that lasted three days. Now, in the old version, it says almost the exact same thing, except that this time it had 'its mouth wide open, its wings beside its body, and fire streaming from its tail.''

'Another deliberate translation change. Much more in keeping with a meteor streaming down,' said the professor.

'Exactly. Now I thought I was onto something. That the ancient religion was so full of holes that I couldn't believe no-one else had spotted it.'

'Mr Yarm, it is getting quite late. So you've proved that there are discrepancies in the Scriptures. Is that really all that important tonight?' Warrad was tired and fed up with all the talk of religion.

'Please, professor, just hear me out on what happened next,' Darrel pleaded. The professor leaned back in his chair. Darrel continued. 'I then wondered what was said about this section of the Scripture in the Garm Hamdra Texts that were found sixty years ago, and indeed, if the events were even mentioned at all.'

'I remember when that discovery was made,' said the old man.

'A lot of the priests at the time were adamant that they were fakes. They must have thought they were heretical in some way.'

'Well, it seems to me that there was never really a cover up, but certainly an accurate translation of the texts was not made public. Even at the museum, I had to fill in a lot of forms before they'd even fetch the translation up from the stacks. I wasn't allowed to Photostat any of it, but I made some notes. The texts not only follow the same story as the old book, but they add far more detail. Also, Harron describes himself not as a priest, as in the Scriptures, but as a wizard or--more accurately--astrologer. But that description, I feel, is an error of the museum translation. From the context of his profession, it seems that he would be better described as a scientist, possibly an astronomer, which is why he noticed the new star in the first place.'

'Now that is more interesting,' the professor chuckled. 'Carry on.'

'The texts were written on small square pieces of papyrus. The translation was made as a facsimile in the same way. Because the pieces weren't numbered, it's extremely difficult to put them in any sort of order, and to know if any are missing or not. When I had read the translation in the order in which it was presented, I found that it made little sense, which is another possible reason why the texts haven't been published. By re-ordering a few of the papyrus pieces, a new, more detailed picture came to light. Firstly, the tail of the 'dragon' describes the tail end rather than an actual tail. Also, the flanks of the dragon which were 'ablaze with lights' in the scriptures were described in the text to be 'covered in lights', which appear to Harron to be 'thousands of skylights', the word skylight also meaning window.'

'What?' asked the professor in surprise. 'Are you telling me that the Dragon is neither a living being nor a dead meteor, but an artificial vessel of some kind?'

'That is exactly what I'm saying. But only because that is what the evidence seems to suggest. In the Texts, the word 'dragon' is not even used. The object is described as simply 'the unknown'. My guess is that if an early draft of the scriptures translated the word as 'unrecognisable' instead of 'unknown', it would have given us a word which phonetically sounded like dragon, a word which loosely fits the evidence. Later, the evidence was changed to fit the name. I think that 'the unknown' was indeed a large alien ship which entered a decaying orbit of our planet and, at the last moment, managed to pull up and escape. I think that it was so huge that it blocked out the light from the sun.'

'An alien ship? What rubbish. Really, Mr Yarm, you surprise me. You're supposed to be a scientist. There are no such things as aliens.'

'You surprise me, Professor Warrad,' said Darrel, shocked. "I have presented the evidence to you. You were willing to go along with the theory that the dragon was a meteorite on virtually no evidence whatsoever. All reports of the 'dragon' record it as 'returning to the heavens', clearly not normal meteorite behaviour. Your meteorite theory is no better than the dragon story.'

'All right, all right. It's obvious that if what you say about the Texts are true than it cannot be a meteorite, but that does not..'

'But professor…'

'But that does not give you reason to jump to your fanciful conclusion.'

'Why do you suddenly doubt my scientific method?' asked Darrel. 'Earlier this evening, you told me that the scientific community applauded my work. My gravitation theories are far more 'fanciful' than the plain evidence I have here.'

'Have you not taken into consideration that it is quite possible that the Garm Hamdra texts are in error? Or even more plausibly, pure fantasy?' the professor said.

'Professor Warrad, I have read those texts. They are nearly two thousand years old. The detail and the life-like way in which they were written means that the author is nothing short of the greatest and most imaginative author that ever lived, while at the same time producing the most un-dramatic and disparate story ever. In addition to that, if you still regard them as 'pure fantasy', why do you take other contemporary or even older texts and tales as being truthful records of history? Even before the Garm Hamdra Texts were discovered, there were very many old versions of the Scriptures. Our classical heritage with the stories of the founders of modern thinking on mathematics and language were drawn from a single text, far older than those discovered at Garm Hamdra. You criticise the priests for their dogma and the closed-minded way they manage to ignore the facts when they are staring them in the face, yet those criticisms can equally be leveled directly at you.'

Warrad said nothing.

'I think I'll go now,' said Darrel. He picked up his file and left the room. Warrad turned his chair to look out of the window. Could it be true, he thought, that the whole of civilisation is founded upon a wrongly interpreted visit from some higher beings, and not upon a mythic tale that never really happened at all?

The House

IMAGINE A HOUSE, A LONELY OLD HOUSE

IN A WORLD OF BLACKNESS RULED BY CREATURES OF THE NIGHT

AND DEMONS FROM AN ANCIENT NIGHTMARE

A FRAIL OLD MAN TOOK UP HIS SUITCASE AND A CANDLE AND LEFT THE COLD, DARK ROOM AT THE FRONT OF THE HOUSE.

THE FIRE'S GRATE WAS EMPTY, AND LOOKED AS THOUGH IT HAD BEEN FOR A VERY LONG TIME

The House

Perception, emotion; we are but interpreters of what we feel and see. Neither can ever be the truth. The true reality could never be constructed in our minds. So our minds interpret it, give it meaning, something tangible. A context. Something we understand. Something we can deal with. For the complete truth would be too much for us.

Imagine a house. A lonely, large, old house, standing in the middle of a wilderness, strewn with rubble and debris, full of evil. Where storms rage and tear at the scarred land. The sky, sombre and inky black, only lit up by the constant flashes of lightning. A world ruled by creatures of the night, demons from an ancient nightmare. Imagine then a light in the window of the lower floor. In the flickering light, a shadow moved.

A frail old man took a coat from the back of a worm-ridden chair and placed it in an old leather suitcase, perched on an old unstable desk. Closing the suitcase, he picked up a candle from the fireplace. The fire's grate was empty and looked as though it had been for a very long time. The white-haired old man left the study and walked down a corridor into a better furnished room. As he put the candle down on the curtain-less windowsill, some leech-like bats flew away from the window. The man closed the door carefully and pulled up the rug in front of the dust-filled hearth. Under the rug was a small silver key. He inserted it in a chest next to the fireplace and opened it to reveal a very antiquated telephone. He wound a handle a few times and then dialled some numbers, placing the ear piece to his ear. He spoke into the mouthpiece. 'Hello? Take it easy...just try to talk slowly...'

Vincent woke. He was lying on a four-poster bed in what looked like a Victorian bedroom. He was scared. He didn't know where he was. He jumped down from the bed and went to the window. Drawing the curtains revealed a heavy blackness outside. A rainless storm raged outside the window. Pressing his face closer to the glass, he got a better view of the ravaged landscape outside. From within every scarred and twisted tree, he thought he saw dozens of pairs of glowing eyes. A branch scraped the window, and Vincent jumped back.

At the same time, the door to the room opened and a young man carrying a candle walked in. 'Who are you?' he said.

'I could ask you the same question,' replied Vincent.

'You mean you don't know why you're here, either?' said the man.

The young man was called Avek. He had woken in the house, too, just as Vincent had, but perhaps an hour or so earlier.

'Where are you from?' asked Vincent.

'You know, that's the funny thing. I can't remember,' said Avek.

'You?'

'I feel as though I should know, but there is a cloud between me and my thoughts,' replied Vincent. 'All I know is that I don't belong here. I'm hungry. Have you found any food?'

'No,' said Avek. "Unless you want to try and catch one of those bats.'

'Bats?' said Vincent.

'The leech like things that cling to the window. They fly off when I open the door to the room.'

'It's getting colder in here. Is there a warmer room? Are there any fires lit?' asked Vincent.

'Let's look downstairs.'

They scouted around the floor below, which was the middle floor the house: a drawing room, a study, a library. The ground floor had a dusty, empty kitchen and a small ballroom. All the rooms had fires. None of which had been used for some time.

'We need to find something to burn,' said Vincent. They were in the library. The walls were lined with shelves of leather bound books. They both pulled a book down.

'We could start with a few of these,' said Avek.

'Look at this one,' said Vincent, reading the gold embossed title on the book. '*The Creatures of Varr*. Do you think that's where we are?' He flicked through the dry tome. On every page, almost every word had been smudged. It was impossible to read.

171

Avek looked in his book, then another. 'Unreadable. And this one, and this.'

They gathered a few of the books together and started ripping and crumpling the dry pages before tossing them into the grate, lighting it with the candle. The pages burned eagerly, producing a lot of smoke. Avek threw a few extra books into the flames.

Vincent started to cough. 'Put it out, put it out!' he spluttered.

The smoke had filled the room. They stamped out the fire. Vincent looked up the chimney. About a foot up, there was a piece of hardboard wood jammed in position.

'It's blocked up!'

Avek ripped at tape that sealed the window-frame and forced the window open. The sound of the storm came in, and the smoke billowed out. They could breathe again. It didn't take long for them to check the other fireplaces. All were similarly boarded up. Avek went to close the window. He saw the glowing eyes and eerie screeches coming from the night. What he couldn't see was a small slug climbing up along the window ledge outside. He slammed the window.

'Why tape up all the windows and board up the chimneys?' he said.

'Have you closed the window?' asked Vincent.

'Obviously,' replied Avek.

'Then why is there a clear draught?'

It was true. The wind whistled into the room. A small hole had appeared in the corner of the window-frame. There, on the inside of the room was a large, leathery slug. They walked over to it. Avek lowered the candle. The thing recoiled.

'How did that get there?' said Avek,

'It appears to have eaten through the window-frame,' said Vincent.

Behind the slug thing, a smaller one had started to slither through the hole. In a panic, they raced out of the room in disgust and slammed the door.

'I think we know why the windows were taped up,' said Vincent.

'Shh! What's that noise?' said Avek. They listened and heard a scraping, crunching noise. Then, at the base of the wooden door they had just slammed shut, the slug thing appeared, munching on the door. It was much larger now, bigger than a hamster. Through the hole, behind it came two more.

'We've got to get rid of it,' said Avek. 'Quick.'

Vincent picked it up by the tail and raced across the hall to the small lavatory. It leaped out of his hand, its teeth biting into Vincent's side. He flicked it off and into the toilet. Vincent flushed it and then looked at his side. The thing had bit through his shirt and there was a deep gouge in his flesh. It bled, but just a little.

Meanwhile, Avek tried to stamp on the other two that had appeared, although more seemed to be crawling through the hole in the door. As they crawled through, they all seemed to head for the spot where he had just stamped his feet. One had taken a bite out of his boot.

Vincent shouted from the toilet. 'Hell, it's drank all the water in the toilet!' he shouted.

The thing was now as large as a fat cat. It flopped out of the toilet bowl onto the floor. Grabbing a towel to wrap around his hand, Vincent slammed the toilet door.

'It's biting through that door now!' yelled Avek.

The thing was as big as a small dog now. Although the creatures resembled slugs, the men could now see they had dozens of short claw feet, a mouth with very sharp teeth, and two large, glowing eyes. Vincent and Avek ran downstairs to the kitchen.

'What are we going to do?' said Vincent.

'I've got a theory,' said Avek. "I think the creatures head for sound. I think they hone in on sounds.'

'A bit far-fetched,' said Vincent.

'Think about it,' said Avek. "We slammed a door, they went for it. I stamped my foot, they went for the spot.'

'So what are we going to do? There are plenty of them outside, so we can't go out.'

'Can we find something to kill it with?'

'Like what? We haven't found anything. Perhaps we can tie a bell on its tail and it'll eat itself,' said Vincent.

'But where do we get a bell?'

They heard a shuffling noise and reduced their talk to a

whisper as one of the things shuffled up to the kitchen door and then stopped.

Vincent and Avek stood very still and quiet. The candle Avek was carrying had now run very low. It went out. As it did so, the shuffling started again. Vincent picked up a small pan and threw it over the creatures head. It hit the stone floor with a clang. The thing turned around and headed for the pan. When it got there, it began to eat it.

'Christ, the thing can eat metal!' said Avek.

'But it proves you're right,' said Vincent, grabbing more pots and pans. 'I've an idea. Make a noise and let's go upstairs.'

They clomped their feet so that the beast would follow them. They met five others on the stairs, all of which turned to follow, too. The larger one was quicker and ate the smaller ones on its way up the stairs.

Back in the library, Vincent said, 'Ok, open the window.'

'What?' said Avek.

'Open the window!'

Avek did as he was told and Vincent threw the pots and pans out of the window. They made a clattering as they hit the ground below. Vincent and Avek froze. Sure enough the large creature entered the room and clambered out of the window and down the wall to the source of the noise. Avek silently closed the window again. They left the library, closing what was left of the door softly and went back downstairs. But there on the landing was one slug that the larger creature had missed. It was the size of a rat and had heard them coming. Vincent and Avek hadn't noticed that it wasn't quite as dark as it had been. Light had been coming in through a landing window, but a distant cloud must have moved out of the way as the bright morning sun of dawn suddenly shone in on the landing floor. The creature screeched and convulsed. Rather like the effect salt has on a slug, the beast gurgled into a mass of disgusting goo.

'Feeding on sound, destroyed by the light,' said Vincent.

They both went downstairs and stripped the tape away from the kitchen door and opened it. Outside it was a winter's morning.

'Why are we here?' said Avek.

'What do you remember now?' asked Vincent.

'The phone rang, I think.'

'Me, too. But I'm sure that was a dream,' said Vincent. "I was dreaming and answered the call, in a dream. Or that's how it felt.'

'No, the phone didn't ring. I rang it,' said Avek. "That's right. I opened the chest and took out the phone. I called you.'

'Something's not right here,' muttered Vincent. "Something that eats sound but hates light. And I can't remember who I am...' Vincent looked down at his side that had been bitten. There was no wound. His shirt wasn't even torn.

'Hello? Take it easy... just try to talk slowly...' said a voice.

Vincent opened his eyes. He was in a room. A white room. In a hospital bed. The doctor leaned over him.

'You'll be pleased to know, the operation has been a success,' said Doctor Avek. 'The tumor in your kidney has been removed and we've found no other trace of the cancer. You made it Vincent!'

The Curse

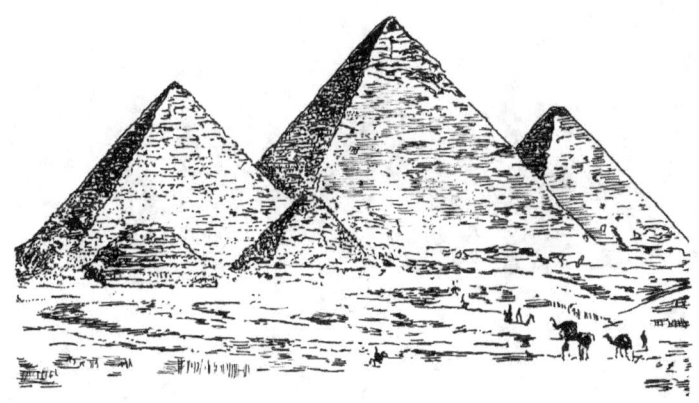

The Curse

The light from the torch made macabre shapes in the yellow cave. Mike Dawson was disappointed. He had expected a cave full of jewels and treasure from centuries past. Instead, there was a cave, dry, musty and sandy just like the surface outside. The torch revealed dark circles in the wall. There were entrances to a honeycomb of passages. The place was like a giant rabbit den. He headed to one of the dark portals, and just inside was an archway on the right, with steps leading down. In the other nearest tunnel entrances were similar arches. But this first one stood out. An excited tingle went down his spine as his torch made out an engraved inscription in the arch above the passage, even though the pictograms did not register consciously in his brain.

The sand crunched underfoot on the stone steps as he descended into the dark, his eyes straining into black space. His ears whined with the noise of total silence. He felt cooler and cooler as the sleeping air, undisturbed for millennia, flowed past him.

After descending maybe twenty feet, he reached the bottom. He stood in a paved crypt. The room was square, and the walls were rough-hewn where smooth plaster had previously adorned it. Now the plaster lay broken on the floor as ugly chunks of rubble and dust. As he moved around the debris, a deafening sound fired off his adrenaline and he swung round. A small section of plaster had fallen to join the rest on the floor. Mike walked over to the newly fallen piece. The plaster was painted red with stylised images of people doing jobs, carrying things and so on.

There was nothing else in the room. Again, no treasure, no storage jars, nothing. At the far side was a small rectangular doorway leading into a further blackness. Mike made his way over carefully. Inside this smaller chamber was a large stone sarcophagus. It was topped with a stone slab, twisted slightly ajar. Mike cleared some of the debris off this lid and put his torch down. He attempted to slide it further to look inside. A sudden rumbling made the torch wobble and then fall off the lid onto the floor with a crash. The light went out. Mike groped around on the floor. He found it and gave it a shake. The front glass was broken, but the torch still worked.

He tried again to move the lid, putting the torch down once again. It was heavy, but moved just enough for him to shine the torch inside to see the contents. It was too tight to reveal anything in the corner of the sarcophagus, so he squeezed his hand with the torch inside to get a good look. The angle was too awkward for his wrist, and he dropped the torch inside. The light went out again. Mike was in the dark once more.

Cross with himself for such foolishness, he heaved at the lid with the hope to move it enough to reach inside and retrieve the torch. The lid came unstuck this time and slid with ease, all the way off the top of the stone box and crashed over the other side of it onto the floor of the vault. A rumbling noise began again, and plaster and dust rained down on his head. He tried to make his way back into the antechamber when a large crash brought the room down ahead. Mike could see nothing. Feeling his way around, he could feel only large rocks and boulders blocking the exit. Then a further crash nearly deafened him as the small vault room he'd just left was destroyed by rubble. Mike was alone, in the dark, in the dusty rubble, coughing what little air remained.

It was two weeks before a group of archeologists and police found the yellow cave. They'd heard rumours about illegal treasure hunters in the area, and when a hotel bill in Cairo had gone unpaid, a team was put together to find the missing man.

The party of ten stood in the sandy cave.

'Look here,' said an American, looking through an archway.

'Steps leading down.' He shone his torch down the stone steps. 'Leading nowhere. Just ends in a pile of rubble.'

'What's that above?' said an English voice, pointing to the inscription above the arch.

An Egyptian, a member of the National Centre of Antiquities came forward. 'Let me see,' she said. 'This place was to be the tomb of a prince, we know that much. But it was never used and was closed up and all but forgotten until now. But I've never seen an inscription such as this before.'

'Why? What does it say?' someone asked.

'Is it a curse?' the American added.

'Of sorts,' replied the Egyptian. 'It reads simply, 'Danger. Unsafe structure. Keep out."

Don't Play
with Fire

Don't Play
with Fire

'I can't ask her. You ask her,' said Graham.

'Why do I have to ask her?' replied Phil. 'You'll never get anywhere if you're so shy you can't even talk to her. It's your room. We'll all be there.'

'I know, but, well, I don't want it to look suspicious.'

'Oh well, all right then,' sighed Phil. 'I'll ask her. You get the others.'

Graham paused for a moment. 'What if she won't come?'

'She will, man. We'll all be there. It's just a laugh, isn't it? Don't be so serious.'

'You remember what we're going to do, don't you? Just as we rehearsed,' Graham said hesitantly.

'Look, it'll be smooth. You get Billy, Julia and Jane,' said Phil.

'Jane's not in, and Billy's not coming,' said Graham emphatically.

'What's up with him?'

'I don't want him to know. He won't like the idea of the Ouija board. You know what he's like. He'll probably spook us up like he usually does. Now make sure she comes or this will be a total waste of time.'

Phil was beginning to get slightly frustrated with Graham's panic driven determination. Why couldn't the man just go and ask her out? The girl lives in the same house for Christ sake, he thought. Phil never had any problems with girls. It had all come very easily to him. He didn't fancy Rachel though, but come to think of it, he hadn't even considered fancying her. Oh that's right, he remembered as he bounded down the narrow staircase to her ground floor room. She doesn't like me. I could never fancy someone who didn't like me. He didn't bother knocking on her door. He just waltzed straight in, calling her name as if he was talking to his sister.

Rachel didn't suspect anything. Graham, Phil, Julia and Rachel all sat in Graham's room on the third floor around a small table upon which Graham had meticulously laid out a circle of cards. Each card had a letter of the alphabet drawn on it except two which had the words 'yes' and 'no'. In the centre of the circle was an upturned wine glass.

'What do we do?' asked Julia excitedly. She was the youngest of the household and the only first-year student in the house.

'We all put our hands on the glass,' said Graham with authority.

'What, like this?' said Julia, thinking the whole thing was one big joke.

'Don't mess about, Julia,' said Graham seriously.

'Yes, Julia, please be much, much more serious,' said Phil,

mocking Graham. 'You're just not serious enough.'

'Look, don't ruin this,' said Graham.

'OK, man, what do we do now?' said Phil sensibly.

'We have our hands on the glass like this, and we ask if there's anybody there, and then we ask a question.'

'What sort of question?' asked Rachel.

'Oh, anything,' replied Graham.

'Is there anybody there?' said Phil in a mocking voice. 'Is there anybody there?'

Julia burst into fits of giggles. She, too, did the funny voice, trying to pitch her voice as low as possible. 'Is there anybody bare?' she said. This time she, Phil and Rachel burst out laughing. Only Graham remained composed.

'This is hilarious,' giggled Julia. 'Someone ask something interesting then.'

'Phil's got a question,' said Graham after a pause for the sniggering to die down. 'Haven't you Phil?' he added through his teeth, kicking Phil from under the table.

Phil muffled a yelp. 'Oh yes. I've got an idea. Let's find out the name of the person who each of us is going to snog next,' said Phil, as if he'd been practising the line all week, which he had.

'What a good idea,' exclaimed Graham.

'Don't be so stupid,' said Rachel.

'Oh come on, Rachel,' teased Julia. 'It's only a bit of fun.'

'Who shall we start with?' asked Graham, trying to act as

nonchalant as possible and failing miserably.

'I think Rachel,' said Phil and, before Rachel could protest, the three of them were all concentrating on the glass.

The glass moved to 'G'

'Mmm, that's an interesting start,' said Phil. 'What could that mean?'

Julia started giggling again.

'You're pushing it,' said Rachel as the glass moved over to 'R'.

'I'm not,' said Phil and took his hand off the glass as it moved over to 'A'.

Julia quickly caught on to what the other two were doing, and she and Graham continued to spell out Graham's name. Julia was in fits of laughter and could hardly keep her hand on the glass. Phil was sniggering. Graham had the sort of look upon his face that said that a carefully thought out chat-up line had gone horribly wrong. Graham wasn't the sort of person who could hide his feelings very well.

'What a load of rubbish,' said Rachel at last, taking her hand off the glass. She saw the humour in the situation now and grinned knowingly across at Graham who looked down at the table. 'I've had enough of this. I'm going to put the kettle on. Cup of tea, Julia?'

'Yes please,' said Julia, out of breath from laughing.

'I'll have a coffee,' said Phil as Rachel opened the door.

'I'm not getting you anything,' she said jokingly and went downstairs.

'You git,' said Graham to Phil.

'Oh come on, mate. It was only a laugh.'

'Oh, let's carry on,' said Julia, ignoring them. They all put their hands back on the glass. 'Let's ask...' she paused to think of a good question. 'Let's ask who's going to die first out of us lot.'

'All right,' said Phil.

'I don't think that's such a good idea,' said Graham.

'What's with you, man?' Phil said as they noticed how the tone of the conversation had suddenly changed.

The door swung open and all three jumped. It was Billy. Julia and Phil erupted into fits of laughter again.

'You scared the life out of me,' said Graham.

'I hope not,' said Billy seriously. 'What do you think you're doing?'

'Just messing about,' said Phil. Their hands were still holding onto the glass.

'You're not doing what I think you're doing?' asked Billy, even more seriously, stepping into the room. As he did so, the glass moved sharply to 'P'.

'Hey, don't push it so hard,' said Graham.

'I'm not,' said Phil. The glass moved to 'H'.

'You two must be pushing it, because I'm not,' said Julia. The glass slid over to the letter 'I'.

'Oh come on, this isn't funny Graham,' said Phil, slightly more worried now. The glass jerked quickly over to the 'L' and then to the centre of the table again.

'Phil,' said Billy matter-of-factly. 'What was that the answer to?'

Phil went pale and snatched his hand from the glass. 'Tell me you were moving that.'

Julia wasn't laughing now, but she was still in a jovial mood, unlike everyone else in the room. 'What's the matter with you lot?'

'You idiots,' said Billy. 'Who have you made contact with?'

'We don't know,' said Graham, half ashamed and half annoyed at Billy's apparent superiority over the situation.

Suddenly the glass started moving again. This time with only Julia and Graham's hands on it. Very quickly it spelled out 'D', 'E', 'V' and then after a brief pause 'I', 'L'. Julia snatched her hand away and covered her mouth.

'You've got to stop this right now,' shouted Billy, too scared to snatch either the glass or Graham away from the table.

'The glass is hot,' said Graham. Condensation seemed to form under the up-turned glass. It started moving again, even quicker this time.

'Let go you fool!' yelled Billy. Phil and Julia were frozen in fear. The glass dashed back and forth across the circle with Graham's hand on top of it. It was repeatedly spelling out 'RACHEL, RACHEL, RACHEL'.

Graham eventually pulled his hand away and jumped to his feet, knocking his chair over. As he did so, a continuous gurgling scream came from downstairs. Billy was first out of the door. The others followed.

They all piled into the kitchen to find Rachel on the floor, still screaming. Billy quickly went over to the sink and turned the kettle off at the mains. Rachel's screams had turned into sobs.

'I, I put the kettle on.' Her words were punctuated with sobbing and shaking.

'Get a blanket, quick,' snapped Billy to the others. Julia ran off to get one.

'As I switched it on, I got a shock.' She erupted into tears and sobs again.

Julia returned and put the blanket around her. 'It's all right,' she said.

'What caused it?' Phil asked Billy.

Billy had a quick look at the kettle. 'Water on the switch, bare wiring, I don't know,' he replied, staring upwards in deep thought.

'Do you think you're all right, or shall we get a doctor?' said Graham.

'I'll be all right now,' Rachel replied.

'Where's the glass?' Billy said to Phil.

'What?'

'The glass. What happened to the glass?'

'It's still up there,' said Graham. 'Why?'

'If you've done what I think you've done and opened a channel for a base spirit to get through, the channel is still open until you smash that glass.'

Billy raced back upstairs, Graham followed. Phil shrugged at Julia and then went up, too. The glass was still there, on the table where they had left it.

'Smash it,' said Billy.

'Go on, Phil,' said Graham.

'I'm not touching that thing again,' Phil said, keeping close to the bedroom door.

Graham went over to the table and picked up the glass carefully.

'Come on. Smash it!' Billy said impatiently. Graham dropped the glass unceremoniously on the carpet. It didn't break.

'Oh, what was that supposed to be? Throw it,' said Billy.

Graham picked up the glass again and threw it hard at the floor. Again it didn't break.

'Throw it out of the window,' said Phil.

Billy quickly opened the window. Graham picked up the glass again and threw it hard straight out of the window.

'It'll have landed on the road,' said Phil.

'I didn't hear anything,' said Billy. They all peered out of the window.

'Can you see it?' asked Phil.

'We're not going to be able to see it from here in the dark, are we? We'll have to go outside,' said Billy.

'No, look,' spluttered Phil astonished. 'There it is!'

'Where?' asked the others. All three squeezed their heads out of the small window, hoping to get a good view.

'Down there,' said Phil quietly.

They looked vertically down, and true enough, there on the windowsill of the room below stood the wine glass, intact.

'I don't believe it,' said Graham,

'We've still got to get it,' said Billy as he dashed from the room.

Moments later, he knocked on Jane's door. Then he remembered that she wasn't in and tried the door. It was open, thankfully. He tip-toed over to the window, opened it, reached outside for the glass and brought it back inside. As he turned to leave, he tripped on a discarded pile of clothes and dropped the glass. It smashed on contact with the carpet. Graham and Phil appeared at the door.

'Someone get a dustpan and brush to get rid of this,' Billy said.

Breakfast the following morning started at half eleven for Billy and Rachel. Phil and Julia had gone to lectures and the others had not emerged from bed yet. Billy was buttering some toast and recounting the tale to the fully recovered Rachel.

'So, if it was the 'devil', why should it spell out your name? It was almost like a warning, telling us that you were in danger. Or maybe it was Graham pushing it since he'd set up the whole scenario just to get your attention.'

'He's got a weird way of going about it. The whole thing's horrible. The house seemed to take on a cold, strange feel. I hope you're right that smashing the glass puts an end to it,' she replied, taking a sip of tea. 'Thanks for fixing the kettle, by the way.'

'And what about Phil?' continued Billy. '"Who will die first?" is what they asked.'

'He was a little freaked out about it,' Rachel said. 'Nearly as much as when you told us that story about the...'

Billy interrupted her. 'We call that 'the story that cannot be told', or at least shouldn't be told in a house that you live in, just in case it comes true. They say that if you tell ghost stories, any passing spirits stop to listen. We don't want a goblin walking about around here, thank you very much.'

'It's funny, really. He says he doesn't believe in this sort of thing, and yet he's the one who gets the most spooked.'
Just then Jane walked in. 'Morning' she said.

'Where were you last night?'

'Oh, I just went into town. I just couldn't get to sleep last night. It was really weird. I was almost convinced there was someone in the room, watching me all the time. In the end, I had to sleep with the light on.'

No one spoke.

'Well?' Jane said surprised. 'Don't you think that's weird?'

Rachel swallowed hard. Billy bit his bottom lip. 'Let me tell you what happened to us last night,' he said.

That afternoon Phil was on his way home. As he crossed the road opposite his house's front door, the road was clear, and he stepped out. From out of nowhere came a large, black lorry, blaring its horn. Phil's instincts took over and the sudden adrenalin rush shot him across the road, up the steps and through his front door. Then he remembered the Ouija prophesy. He went quietly into the kitchen and sat down. No-one else was home, it seemed. Putting down his bag, he reached into his jacket pocket for a crumpled cigarette packet and thrust the last remaining cigarette into his mouth. He patted his pockets for his lighter. It must be in my bag, he thought. Never mind. He went over to the cooker and reached for the large box of matches. He fished one with a pink head out from the majority of burnt used ones in the box and was about to strike it when he stopped. Something was wrong. There was a hissing. He looked down at the cooker. The gas was on.

Phil twisted the dial on the cooker to off as the cigarette dropped from his mouth. He was conscious of the smell of gas now. After opening the windows, he went cautiously to his room and stayed there until the others came home.

Later that night, Julia went up to her room on the top floor. She pulled back the duvet and was surprised to see four drawing pins arranged in a square in the centre of the bed. Looking up she could see that they had been arranged directly below the corners of the loft hatch that was above the bed. Before she had a chance to do anything else, the door suddenly slammed shut and the light went out. Someone's playing tricks on me, she hoped. She knew that everyone else was down in the kitchen still. Maybe someone followed her upstairs. She opened the door, thinking that the door slam had helped to blow the bulb. As the light from the tiny landing crept into her open doorway, she saw that the old brown bakelite light switch was in the off position. She flipped it on again and the light came on.

Puzzled, but not worried, she went back over to her bed to examine the drawing pins again. Then exactly as before, the door slammed and the light went off. This time it was too much, she swung the door open and flew downstairs into the relative safety of the kitchen with the others.

Phil and Julia had recounted their stories to Billy, Graham, Jane and Rachel.

'I hope you're not blaming me for all this,' said Graham, conscious that he had been left out of the recent conversation.

'Well, you were the idiot who started playing with things you don't understand,' said Billy.

'Oh, and I suppose you do understand it all. I suppose you've got an explanation for it all. I bet you're going to tell us how the gas was left on and why those drawing pins turned up in Julia's bed,' Graham replied sharply.

'They weren't the first things to turn up in Julia's bed

mysteriously,' said Phil.

'Phil!' said Julia, embarrassed of her frequent and numerous short-term boyfriends.

'No, I don't know what's going on. All I know is that something is going on,' replied Billy.

'I still feel quite odd,' said Jane. 'There's something not quite right.'

'It does feel quite cold,' suggested Graham. 'Isn't that supposed to be the sign of spectral visitation?'

'Spectral incursion is a better term. Incursion, as in attack. You're right, though. It is cold.'

'Yes, but it is February,' said Rachel, not taken in with all the talk of spirits.

'We need protection,' said Billy firmly.

'What do you mean?' asked Phil.

'Psychic protection. Just in case there is something here.'

'What, like the Exorcist, you mean?' Phil asked.

'Not necessarily at this stage' said Billy.

'Oh, come on,' said Graham disbelievingly. 'A few strange coincidences and you think you're a ghost hunter.'

'You saw what happened with the glass,' said Billy.

'Yes, but it didn't mean anything. You're crazy Billy. You're a nutter, a freak merchant. I'm going to bed.' Graham made for the door.

'Make sure the bogey man doesn't get you,' said Julia jokingly.

Graham gave her a sarcastic smile and left.

In less than an hour, they had all gone to bed.

There were no incidents during the next two days and conversation seemed to get back to more ordinary and mundane topics.

One afternoon, Rachel was alone in the kitchen doing the washing up. Music was playing from the small stereo almost hidden behind dirty dishes and junk on the kitchen table. She emptied the dirty, tepid water from the washing up bowl and stopped to listen more closely to the stereo. There was a voice, singing along to the song. It was slightly distorted, as if the radio wasn't tuned in properly, a kind of eerie grating tuneless voice. Rachel felt goose-pimples forming all over her, and a shiver ran down her spine. Someone must have recorded over the tape, she thought. She stepped over to the stereo to stop the tape and get rid of the disgusting creepy voice, only to find that it was the radio which was on. The voice was 'singing' along to the radio. She quickly turned the radio off in fright and ran back to the sanctuary of her own room. The next day it was Phil who was alone in the kitchen. He was reading a newspaper and felt as though someone was behind him, eyes burning into the back of his head. He wanted to turn around, but dared not, frightened of what he might see. Eventually he turned around slowly to see the door to the larder was slightly ajar. The larder was a tiny room off the kitchen, lined with shelves where the household kept all their packets and tins of food. Phil quickly shut the door and sat down again. It still wasn't right. He fished in the top drawer and pulled out a reel of masking tape and proceeded to seal the door, becoming more frantic all the time. When the door had been sealed shut, he went upstairs to his room, put the television on, and hoped that the others would come back soon.

'Why in there?' Billy asked Phil after tea. 'There was no-one in there. There's hardly any room in there for anyone.'

'I just don't know,' Phil said. 'I was convinced someone or something was in there.'

They were the only two in the kitchen.

'Let's have a look in there,' said Billy, stripping the tape away.

'I'd rather not.'

Billy opened the door. Inside was the same old larder, full of the same old packets and tins. 'Come in. There's nothin interesting here.'

Phil stayed outside. Billy tapped the walls. The first two were solid enough, but the one to the right gave a hollow sound.

'There's something behind this wall,' he said and began to move the stuff off the shelves on the hollow wall onto neighbouring shelves. 'Come and look at this,' he said as he dismantled the shelving.

Phil poked his head round the corner.

'There's a door here!' exclaimed Billy. 'A door that's been painted over, look.' Sure enough, the outline of a door could be seen quite clearly now. 'Pass me a knife'.

Phil brought a knife, and Billy used it to score the paint around the door. 'There's no handle anymore. We could pry it open. Pass me something thick. I don't know, one of those heavy forks.' Phil brought the fork, and soon the door was open. Behind it lay a cold dusty darkness.

'Candles,' said Billy.

'I'll get them, but I'm not going in there.'

'I think it leads down to a cellar,' said Billy ignoring him.

Upstairs, Rachel and Julia sat on the bed watching television in Julia's room. Rachel turned to Julia. 'Is that heater on? It's freezing in here.'

Julia looked across at the five bar heater. It was on full. 'Can you feel something?' she asked.

'Yes, I feel cold,' replied Rachel, pulling the duvet around her a bit more.

'No, something else,' asked Julia again.

'Yes,' replied Rachel slowly, as if listening to something very faint. 'There's someone here.'

They both slowly looked around the room. There was no-one to be seen.

'I think her name's Mary,' both girls said at once, then stopped to stare at each other in disbelief.

In the larder, Billy had a candle and was precariously venturing down the stone steps into darkness.

Phil watched from the top. 'What can you see?' he whispered.

'Nothing yet,' replied Billy. He descended further until the candlelight found a purchase on a vast collection of strange-shaped objects which filled the musty, shadowy room which was about the same size as the area of the house. The walls were made of crumbled brick. As Billy's eyes got used to the shapes, he managed to make out what they were: furniture of all shapes and sizes, all covered in dark cloths, rugs and carpets rolled up, picture frames and other similar objects. In one corner was a rocking horse, and in another a hat stand. All the items look extremely old and incredibly dusty.

Billy stepped over to a table. On it was a gas lamp next to a large pile of books. Billy felt that he had walked into a time capsule, or a museum storeroom. He felt more curious than frightened. That changed when his candle went out and he felt a little girl's hand in his. He froze. The hand was still there. He looked slowly round into darkness. Snatching his hand back, he pelted back up the stairs, nearly knocking Phil over. He slammed the cellar door shut, and the larder door, too.

'What happened?' asked Phil.

'There was someone there,' replied Billy, out of breath.

'A little girl with a torn dress,' said Phil calmly.

'What?' said Billy astonished. 'What makes you think that?'

'I don't know. I just felt it as you ran up the steps. The feeling went away as soon as you shut the larder door.'

Rachel and Julia entered the kitchen to get themselves a cup of tea. Julia put the kettle on while Rachel went over to the larder to get the tea bags out. She tried the handle and noticed the masking tape that sealed up the door. 'What's going on here?' she asked.

'What's that?' asked Julia's, not turning round.

Rachel looked over at the kitchen table. It was stacked high with all their food from the larder.

'Someone's emptied the larder. Why?' said Julia.

Rachel peeled off the tape and opened the larder door. Sure enough, all the shelves were empty. 'That's odd,It's a spectral incursion' she said, closing the door.

'Maybe there's an ant nest in there or something,' offered Julia.

Rachel went to the bottom of the stairs and shouted for Billy, Phil and Graham. It was Phil who answered and bounded down the stairs. The girls asked him about the emptying and sealing up of the larder.

'There's a cellar under there. Billy and I think it's haunted. He's gone to the library to see if he can find out any history about this street.'

Julia thought the story was mildly amusing. Rachel acted as though she thought it was utter nonsense and demanded that Phil put all the packets, tins and jars back on the shelves. Since Rachel's wrath was a little scarier than any apparition, Phil complied.

Rachel was worried, however. She hadn't been able to explain the strange feeling in Julia's room, or anything else for that matter. The girls finished making their tea and went back upstairs to the television.

Later that afternoon, Billy returned.

'What did you find out?' Rachel asked.

'Nothing much. Only that this area has always been the poor end of the city. There was a leper colony around here about eight-hundred years ago. The librarian referred me to some books in the Bodleian Library that are specifically about this area. We might find out something there. I'll go tomorrow. I've been thinking about this whole thing and have been asking a few people about magic. I've got to talk to Graham. Something's worrying me about him.'

'We told him about the sightings. He said he wanted to find out who the spirits could be by doing the Ouija board again,' said Phil.

'What!' exclaimed Billy. 'The fool.'

'I though he didn't believe all the talk of ghosts,' said Rachel.

'That's what first caused me alarm,' Billy replied. 'I knew he was lying. He was just as curious as us, if not more so. I think he knows more than he's letting on. Come on, let's find him.' Phil and Julia followed Billy upstairs.

Jane was alone in her room. She was working on a drawing for her art project at college. She'd been feeling quite uninspired when suddenly felt the compulsion to draw a figure. The drawing became more and more detailed as Jane became more and more engrossed in the image. She was not normally one for drawing imaginative drawings, preferring to draw or paint from life or construct abstract collages. With this drawing, she felt different, guided almost, or as if she had to hurry and finish the drawing before the inspiration left her, like as if she was desperately trying to remember something before it was forgotten.

At last the drawing was finished. It looked quite odd, quite dark and disturbing. It showed a figure of a woman with long dark hair, one hand over her mouth, the other outstretched. The thick dark graphite marks swirled chaotically around the rest of the paper. But Jane still wasn't happy with it. Something was missing. She reached for her small plastic toolbox that contained her paints and crayons. She pulled out a handful of coloured pastels and began adding dramatic swipes of colour to the lower half of the picture. Thick orange, yellow and red lines she added, and then stopped to look again at the picture that she had created. Yes, that's right. It's finished now, she thought.

Billy burst into Graham's room without warning. Graham sat at the table in the centre of his room and, as the others had suspected, he had his hands on another glass. He looked up at the intruders with mild disinterest, as if he didn't recognise them. He then began to burble unintelligible gibberish at them. Billy stepped back, pushing Phil and Julia back out of the room.

'What are you doing?' asked Phil.

'He didn't see you, but I think he saw me.' Billy said.

'What do you mean?' asked Julia.

'He's possessed. I'm sure of it now. The entity that's inside him saw me. It knows who I am and what I want to do.'

In his hand, Billy held a large hammer. He opened the door again and stepped through. Suddenly the door slammed into him, trapping him between it and the door frame and knocking the breath out of him. He squeezed out into the room and the door slammed shut behind him. The room appeared to be full of a thick dark cloud. It wasn't quite visible but was there none-the-less. Graham's face which was frozen still, staring at him in indignation. The bulb didn't light up the whole room. It seemed to create a shaft of light downwards in which could be seen thousands of tiny dust particles shining like stars.

Billy stepped up to the table and raised the hammer over the glass. Books and other objects jumped off the shelves and flew towards him, striking him on his head. He brought the hammer down on the glass, breaking it, and the table. Graham fell to the floor and the room was bathed in normal light once more.

That night, Graham slept in Rachel's room, and Rachel stayed with Julia in hers. They all had a surprisingly restful sleep. It was Billy who had disturbing dreams. He dreamt he was driving along in the passenger seat of a car. He suddenly became aware of a horrible diabolical feeling, and all the hairs on the back of his neck stood on end. He felt sure he was about to see a ghost and looked out of the car window to see what was there. He disappointingly saw nothing, and then turned to see that it was Jane who was driving the car.

'It's a spectral incursion,' she said, with worry on her face. 'We'd better get off the road.' Up ahead on the right was a church. 'We'll be safe here,' she said.

The car swerved to the right into the church's lane. The motion of the car caused Billy to turn his head round and look in the back seat. There sat two figures. They were two men dressed in brown old-fashioned suits. Both men looked at him, their ghoulish faces grinning. Billy screamed.

He woke up in a deep sweat, panting. It was a dream. No, it was more than a dream. Something has been here, but now it's gone. His door was open. He sat up, alarmed. Someone was there. He looked to the side of his bed to see Jane standing there.

'I could hear you panting and breathing very heavily from next door,' she said. 'I knew something must be wrong, so I came in and prayed by your bedside.'

'Thank you,' he said.

The next morning Jane brought the drawing to show the others.

'I drew this last night. I don't know why.'

Julia and Rachel immediately said in unison, 'That's Mary.'

'How do you know that?' asked Jane.

'She's looking for her baby,' added Julia.

They all looked at the picture again. It quite clearly showed a woman trying to force her way through flames, one hand over her mouth trying to stop herself being suffocated from the smoke.

'Well I'm going to the library today. I'll see if I can find out anything else,' said Billy.

That evening he returned. The whole household was eager to hear what he'd found.

'This street and the two adjacent ones were the site of a cemetery for a church at the top of the hill which has long since gone. That big house at the top was built on the site where the vicarage once was,' Billy recounted. 'You can tell that this area has had some spiritual past by looking at the names of the streets.'

'Like Divinity Road,' said Graham.

'Yes,' continued Billy, 'and Bartholomew street. Saint Bartholomew was the name of the old church. Nearby we've got Magdalene Road and St Mary's Road, named after Mary Magdalene and Mary, the mother of Jesus. Old churches were often built on sacred sites that could go back even further in history. We might find that this area is susceptible to spiritual phenomena because it is on the cross-roads of two intersecting ley-lines.'

'So, our house was built on graves?' asked Julia in disgust.

'Not directly. The time spans we're talking here are huge. On top of the cemetery was built a street of houses, yes, but not the ones that are here today. If you look at the house two doors down, you can see that it is much older. In fact that house was built in the 1300's. Our house was built in about 1820.

'The older houses on this row are actually listed buildings. The house that stood where our house is now was burnt down in 1696. I think that the foundations and the cellar have survived from the original building. This house and the one next door were simply built on top. I found one book that compiled collected stories of this area. In the burnt wreckage of the house, they found the body of a woman who, eye witnesses said entered the house while it was on fire. In the cellar, they found the remains of a little girl, who, they claimed, could have been playing with a tinder box, used to light cigarettes before matches were invented.'

Billy looked sternly at the others. 'So, the ghost of a little girl playing with fire was re-kindled by Graham playing with a very much more dangerous fire three hundred years later. The channel of negative energy and emotions that he opened allowed a whole manner of disjointed images and dismembered consciousnesses to flow through to our level. Whatever we did made contact with initially was right about one thing.'

'What was that?' asked Graham.

'That Phil would be the first to die.'

They all looked at him in astonishment and horror. Billy continued. 'Phil told me when we first met over two years ago that he was born prematurely and was kept in an incubator in intensive care for the first few days of his life.'

'That's right. I'd forgotten about that,' said Phil.

'And during that time, he actually 'died' but was resuscitated by the doctors. Hence, literally he was the first to die out of all of us.'

'All right,' said Graham, 'that may well be the case. But how could a spirit, whoever or whatever it may be, possibly know that?'

'Spirits are all-knowing, you know,' said Phil.

'Possibly,' added Billy. 'Or maybe the spirit that was guiding the glass was actually Phil's, who did know. You know how the theory goes: that although we exist in physical form here, the real 'us', our true self is somewhere else, interconnected with everyone else's spirit form in a collective sub-conscious. That could explain how some of us picked up certain vibrations, such as Rachel and Julia's feeling of the mother looking for her child, and Jane's painting.' He continued, 'That's another reason why the Ouija board, and other forms of dubious magic, is literally like playing with fire; the people in the circle are opening the channel to other consciousnesses through themselves, leaving their bodies open to possession by another entity. The most frightening thing about such possession, which makes me think how lucky we've been, is that such channelling always opens an obvious door into the spirit realm, to a low level where evil entities are ready and waiting to come through to our world. That's why I was attacked in my dream. Whatever it was, it had discovered the open channel, but hadn't managed to come though totally. It saw me as an obstacle. I was trying to stop Graham from doing the Ouija board again. All the time, Graham was in the most danger. He had tried not only to use a magical ceremony without realising its full potential, but he had gone into that ceremony wanting something for himself. To use magic for one's own gain is the nature of black magic. To use magic to influence someone else's will--in this case Rachel's--is the most terrifying use of black magic.'

'Yes, but I didn't know,' said Graham. 'I wasn't to know that the Ouija board was for real. I thought it was just a game. I didn't mean any harm by it, not to Rachel or anybody. You seem to know so much about it. How come you're not in danger? You read those books on Tarot and that visualisation stuff that you go on about. Isn't that dangerous, too?'

'There's nothing wrong with reading books. There's no danger in knowledge. To be fore-warned is to be fore-armed, but to meddle with things that are unknown and not understood is extremely dangerous. If the little girl had understood the terrifying properties of fire, she would not have experimented with a tinder-box in the cellar of a house that was made primarily from wood leading to her and her mother's death and the destruction of the house. In fact, knowing the consequences of such action, she would have probably left fire well alone.'

The Escape

The Escape

Rongar ran blindly, desperately through the field. The mud splashed up his legs, and the hail tore at his flesh, but he ran on. The edge of the field came in sight. His thoughts were of only one thing: escape. Why he had been kept prisoner, he could not tell. He had not been interrogated, just simply confined to a cell. He had killed many of the ugly, tiny creatures that had held him captive during his escape.

Then he stumbled on the thick, uneven surface and stopped, panting, his heart pumping wildly. The field was surrounded by rolls of barbed wire, sharp and shiny. He paused. The hail turned to snow. Grasping the wire in his hands, he bit through it. Blood trickled out from his mouth. He pushed his way through the cold, spiny steel cage, biting various obstinate wires until he was through. He ran on again.

The air seemed to oscillate with a faraway 'boom,boom' which became progressively nearer. Rongar fell, got to his feet, and fell again. He looked up. What he saw made him freeze with fear. A giant silver crab hung in the air above him. The 'boom boom' noise emanated from it. Rongar felt as though his skull was collapsing. 'Boom,boom.' He fainted.

Commander Ryder walked up to the motionless figure which, even when spread-eagle on the ground, dwarfed him. The giant green claw that was Rongar's right arm twitched involuntarily.

'Okay', said Ryder at last. 'Doctor, give him an injection to keep him under. I want to make sure he doesn't come round before we can get him back to the compound.'

'It should have been slaughtered straight away,' said a voice.

'You know the law as well as I do, soldier,' said the commander. 'This creature may be a maneater, but it's still a living being, who may find us as repulsive as we find him. Now let's get him back to the zoo where he belongs.'

Dissent

Dissent

Geoffrey Sax and Roger Harper could be described as friends even though they only had two things in common: their obstinacy and their closed-minded reluctance to budge one inch from their firmly held beliefs. They disagreed on everything. It was not surprising, then, that Harper had become a research physicist, and Sax a theologian and historian.

It had been ten years since they last met, although their correspondence had been kept up with the occasional letter and the odd phone call, reserved for times when something quite exceptional had occurred in one or the other's lives, which was as rare as their letters were short.

It was something of a surprise, then, for Sax to receive a letter, forwarded to him from his Oxford college, from his old university friend. It took Sax several minutes to decipher the appalling handwriting, and several more to extrude a meaning from the atrocious grammar and spelling. It took rather longer than that for him to come to terms with the fact that Harper had written to him at all, and nearly a week for him to decide to follow the instructions laid out in the letter for an urgent rendezvous at Harper's house in Berkshire.

The letter stated, quite plainly, that he should tell no-one and come immediately, and alone. Now Sax would normally have no intention of following anyone's instructions, especially those of Harper. The simple description in the letter of a 'discovery' would not ordinarily be enough for him to give up a weekend. It was the paragraph that stated that Harper needed his help that really caught his eye. Harper needed him. Those words echoed through Sax's head like an angelic choir. It was not being needed; he was keen to help. No, it was the simple fact that he would be one up on Harper. He would be on top. He had to see what Harper wanted, and then he would consider giving it to him.

Such thoughts of superiority engaged his mind thoroughly during the course of the two-hour journey to Harper's medium sized gothic-looking house on a quiet country road. Sax drove his car up the short gravel drive and got out. Well, this is the right place according to the map, he thought. I can't imagine Harper living here. Much too far from modern civilisation. Then another thought struck him. He can't have changed that much, could he? That thought made him very conscious of his own aging in the past ten years. 'Well, everybody gets a little fatter,' he said to console himself before stepping quietly up to the front door.

The door was opened by an extremely tall, thin and gaunt Harper. He looked down at Sax from the doorway.

'Where have you been?' he asked, as if the two had seen each other every day as a matter of course.

He's trying to get the upper hand already, thought Sax. 'Time hasn't given you any manners?' he said.

'I suppose I should be grateful that you're still alive. I had my doubts,' said Harper.

Sax followed Harper through the old house, into the kitchen and up to a door. Harper opened it revealing steps leading down into darkness.

'Down here,' said Harper, making sure Sax entered the doorway and had navigated three steps in total blackness before turning on the light.

The cellar was cold, but not damp, and quite large. The walls were lined with shelves barely visible behind the jagged jumble of mechanical and electrical clutter, which also lined the corners of the room. The centre of the floor area was clear, however, just as if someone had swept the knee-deep junk to the edges of the room only a few minutes before to reveal a large circle of dirty, oil stained stone floor. In the centre of this cleared area stood a spherical shape made up from pentagonal and hexagonal sides. A few of the pentagon faces had pipes jutting out, in some cases re-entering at another face. Some just curved down like large overflow pipes. The two faces opposite Sax were somehow hinged, one up, one down, a feature Sax thought must be a door of some kind.

'Well?' asked Harper as if Sax should be overjoyed at the sight.

Sax was impressed, whatever the construction was supposed to be. It certainly looked impressive, but he didn't show it. 'What is it?' he asked at last.

'Now, I must ask you, whether you decide to join me or not,

to keep everything you see here completely secret,' said Harper seriously.

'Now wait a minute. If you're after funding for this...this...whatever this is, you've picked the wrong man. My department is way over budget as it is, and my personal funds are virtually non-existent.'

'No, Geoffrey,' said Harper calmly.

That's odd, thought Sax, straining his memory to see if Harper had ever called him by his first name before. He didn't think he had.

'I don't want your money, or anybody's money,' Harper continued.

That's good, thought Sax, who was actually quite well-off.

'I need you for something quite different. Step inside the machine.' Harper beckoned him over to the giant ball.

Sax lowered his head and lifted his legs through the small entrance. Inside was a small rectangular room, much smaller than the outside shape had suggested. Sax wondered what could take up the extra space, but that was just one of the plethora of questions which filled his mind. There were two soft moulded seats, opposite one another. Harper sat down on one and invited Sax to sit in the other. The walls were covered in instruments, switches, and lights. Sitting down, Sax eventually asked the inevitable question.

'All right Harper, what is it?'

'It, my dear fellow, is a Time Machine,' Harper said coolly.

'What?' spat Sax after a disbelieving pause. 'No way.'

'It's true. I know it's true. I've worked for ten years on this project. It's perfect. I've tested it on short trips so far, going back in time a few days, weeks, cautiously at first. The Time Sphere can only go into the past. The future is still untouchable, for the moment at least.' Harper smiled proudly at his little impromptu joke. He continued, 'Even I couldn't really believe I would achieve it.' He paused again, as if looking lovingly into his past. 'My biggest trip was the latest one. That was the trip I had to make before I knew that the experiment was completed, before I could invite you here. I travelled back to ten years ago and gave myself the idea, the plans and all the necessary details to build the machine.'

'That's ridiculous,' said Sax.

'It saved me a lot of time,' said Harper. 'Without my help, it could have taken me fifty years to perfect the theory and the technology needed for such an advanced machine.'

'I don't believe it,' Sax said in astonishment.

'Oh come on now, my old friend. Believe it. It's me. I've done it. What no-one else could dream of doing: I built the perfect tool for studying the past.' Gloating came so naturally to Harper. 'Pick any moment in History. Choose a time everyone thinks they've got stitched up, then come back to the present with information that upsets the entire establishment! Think of it. Bringing back artifacts from the past, slowly, only a few at first. Enough to sell to make us both immensely rich.'

'Surely you mean to publish your research?' said Sax

'Absolutely not!' said Harper in disgust. 'And become surrounded by a media circus, have my machine dissected, its secrets stolen? No. This is mine.' Harper became conscious of being too big-headed. He softened his tone slightly and went on. 'What about the moral dilemma? Here, the secret of time travel is safe. Only we two know of its existence. Like any invention, this machine could be put to diabolic use, don't you agree? With us, it's safe.'

Sax really didn't know quite what to say except, 'Why me? What have I got that I should be 'rewarded' by your invention?'

'My dear fellow,' answered Harper, 'you can choose the destination for our first trip.'

Sax was still astonished and didn't reply. He still wasn't sure if he believed him.

'Come on,' said Harper impatiently. 'You're the historian. What do you want to see? What don't you know? Don't tell me you already know everything. Your religion hasn't drummed every last scrap of curiosity out of you, has it? Has your thirst for knowledge finally been quenched?'

'No, not at all,' retorted Sax, still deep in thought. Before he could reply, Harper continued, stepping back from the machine and turning to face it in admiration.

'Who built the pyramids? We will know. We will be able to see them being built.' He spun round suddenly. 'Don't you see, man? Who was the real King Arthur? Did Richard III really kill his two nephews?' He paused, purely for effect as he had his next line rehearsed. 'Who shot Kennedy?' He went on, 'You can wait there on that grassy knoll. Converse with Shakespeare on inspiration for his works. Visit Atlantis – if it existed, but of course, you would know. You'd be the only one who'd know.'

You offer me, it seems, what I desire most,' said Sax calmly.

'Then there is still some fire in you. Just think: you could return to December 8th 1980, meet John Lennon at his recording studio, and tell him not to go home that night.'

'Oh come on,' said Sax disbelievingly.

'Travel back to Austria in the late twenties and kill an unknown painter...'

'No!' Sax interrupted. 'You cannot go blundering through time changing this and that at your merest whim. What right do we have to dictate history? Has science driven every last scrap of morality out of you?' Sax stood up and stepped out of the machine.

'Don't be a fool, Sax!' came Harper's voice from within the sphere. He stepped out and continued, 'Hitler was single-handedly behind the death of millions. Of course it would be better if he died, unknown and unmissed. I'm sure six million Jews and their surviving families would agree with me.'

'Perhaps' said Sax thoughtfully.

'You're not about to lecture me on the good that came out of the War, are you? You're going to tell me that we'd have no computers, no commercial aircraft, no atomic power.'

'And no atomic bombs,' added Sax.

Harper felt slightly beaten. He wanted to whip Sax into a frenzy, but of course he realised now that he had offered to Sax what he himself wanted. He consciously tried to calm himself down.

'All right. I'm only postulating. Of course you're right.' Harper hated saying that. 'We'll agree not to interfere with the natural flow of history. We'll choose a time that you're familiar with so that we can blend in inconspicuously. We'll be observers only. How about that? What would you wish to observe most? Come on, there must be something.'

Sax didn't need to think hard. It was the first thing that had popped into his head when the suggestion of time travel first appeared to be a possibility. 'The first century' he said quietly.

'Roman Empire, right? That specifies a time, yes, but where?' Harper was no longer ashamed to hide his impatience.

'Somewhere in the Middle East.' Sax paused. 'Galilee. No, Jerusalem.'

'Excellent choice!' beamed Harper, raising his arms in delight.

'All right,' said Sax with resignation. 'Say that we can travel to first century Jerusalem. You'll have to rely on me to speak ancient Hebrew, and even I only know a little of that. I'll certainly sound odd. Maybe their dialect is completely incomprehensible.'

'Then you will have a very interesting job to do. Just think, the only man to speak ancient Hebrew in a first century Jerusalem dialect.' Harper turned back to the machine. 'But don't try to catch me out Sax, I've thought of everything. I've been learning Hebrew,

Greek and even a little Aramaic, to the best of my ability for the past five years.'

Sax looked astonished. 'You predicted my choice of time and place!'

'Naturally,' Harper responded calmly. 'The experiment would be utterly pointless unless I had a real point to prove. What better point to prove, once and for all—that I am right, and you are wrong?'

'I think you'll be in for a few surprises, then,' said Sax, in a failed attempt to get back his upper hand.

'Naturally,' said Harper once again.

Sax paused for thought. Harper's last words only just began to settle in. 'You still haven't answered my question. Why get me involved? Why share this so-called wealth you seem to think the machine will bring with me? Why will travelling to Jerusalem 'prove me wrong'?'

Harper wasn't going to answer. He knew that Sax would realise himself immediately, and he smiled at that fact. Faith was something Harper had never had. It was the one thing Sax had that Harper had always wanted. Now, after another ten years for modern science to convince him that there was simply nothing out there for him to believe in, he had vowed to take away from Sax that which he could not find for himself. First century Jerusalem was the time and place, in his mind, to do that. That is where the reality of Christ, his mission, his life, death and resurrection lay. This time Sax smiled.

Typical scientist, he thought. The worst type of fundamentalist. But a shiver went down his spine. The sheer scale of Harper's mission was reaching him. Somewhere inside his soul was a box marked 'Faith'. Before he arrived here, he was sure it felt like a large solid oak cask. Now it seemed to be a small flimsy cardboard box. Harper meant to open that box and reveal nothing but dust. He shivered again.

'How can you be sure that the time you specify is where the machine will take us?' he asked.

'Simple,' replied Harper confidently. 'The sun's emission of neutrinos is not constant over its surface; different areas give different emissions. Likewise, the Earth's orbit takes us through a range of different distances from the sun. For the past five years, I have been studying these differences and can now calculate the Earth's position relative to the sun fully, in four dimensions. The time travel system has to be linked to the sun because the Earth moves through space around the sun, which is orbiting the Milky Way galaxy, which in turn is hurtling through the universe. We wouldn't want to materialise in deep space, thousands of light years from the Earth.'

'Incredible,' said Sax, not really understanding at all.

Harper walked around the machine, pretending to check on some complicated piece of equipment to make Sax feel much more insignificant than he already felt.

'Now listen to me, Harper,' said Sax, following Harper round the machine. 'I hope you don't have any ideas about changing the course of history and religion by interfering with Christ's mission.'

'If he existed at all,' said Harper without looking up. 'Don't worry,' Harper turned around and grinned inanely. 'We'll turn up to the 'feeding of the five-thousand'. No-one will spot us there.'

Sax didn't know whether to take Harper seriously or not. He now felt that the whole thing was a hoax and a complete waste of his time.

'So I take it that you'll be coming,' said Harper at last.

'I'm still not sure that I believe you.'

'Oh, I think you do. I need to know now because we'll need to complete a lot of complicated preparations.'

'We'll need period dress,' said Sax.

'Done,' said Harper. 'Although I had hadn't calculated on you being—how can I put it?—somewhat fuller, than you once were.'

Sax scowled at him.

'No, what we need to do is pack up the machine and take it over to the desired location in Jerusalem,' continued Harper.

'Can't we just, well, get there in the machine?' asked Sax.

'What do you think this is? You've been reading too much clichéd science fiction. I could have built the machine into an aeroplane, but I didn't, so we'll have to take it there ourselves.'

'But surely as the Earth moves through space around the sun, this point where we are now will line up with ancient Jerusalem,' said Sax, proud of this theory.

'Possibly,' said Harper dismissively. 'But you try doing four dimensional equations, trying to keep all errors to an absolute minimum. Putting the machine in the right place on Earth takes one variable out of the equations.'

It was just short of a year later when the two men finished rebuilding the sphere in a building they had rented on the outskirts of Jerusalem, inside the old city walls. During the year, they had obviously seen each other often, flying over with machine parts packed into the smallest containers possible, sometimes together, and later alone. Harper insisted on paying for the entire enterprise. Even after spending so much time together, they rarely talked about the project other than operational business. Sax never questioned Harper about the plausibility of time travel, even though he still wasn't sure if he believed him. Perhaps Harper had gone mad — he didn't know—but he had certainly been swept along by the whole experiment.

Sax made his way as quickly as he could through the busy market-filled streets to the ramshackle, but very expensive, squat building in which they had built the Time Sphere. He stopped outside to wipe the sweat from his forehead with an equally sweaty forearm, then went down inside into the stone building's cooler interior.

Inside, Harper was making adjustments to various connections on the top of the sphere. He didn't look up. 'You're sure you've got everything?'

'Only just,' replied Sax. 'I got stopped at customs. I knew it would happen sooner or later. They thought I had a bomb.'

'Load the food into the sphere, will you?' said Harper, spanner in hand. 'We'll be able to go this afternoon.'

'So soon?' said Sax, surprised.

'Well, only if you've got nothing better you'd rather be doing,' snapped Harper.

'I thought I should tell my mother where I'll be,' said Sax.

'Don't be ridiculous,' sneered Harper. 'Hello, mum. I'm off to ancient Jerusalem, two thousand years ago. I'll be back in an hour.' Harper climbed down from the rigging. 'We can come back an instant after we've left. We could spend years away, which would only seem like seconds when we return.'

'Oh, I forgot,' said Sax, packing picnic baskets of food and drink into the machine.

It was a few more hours later before they were finally ready. They sat in their seats inside the Time Sphere, opposite one another and dressed in their first century Jewish apparel. Harper closed the octagonal faces that made the entrance hatch and consulted a screen surrounded with controls.

'What now?' asked Sax.

'I've got to make sure that, when we arrive in the past, we won't materialise underground, or on top of someone. The computer is scanning the probability transform for this area for the time we have specified.' He gazed intently at the complex wave-form displayed on the screen. 'I think we'll be all right.' He sat down. 'Do up your seat belt and put these on.' He handed Sax a pair of headphones and put on a pair himself.

'Why?' asked Sax.

'You'll see,' said Harper, fixing his belt in place. Sax did the same. 'We're ready.'

'As ready as we'll ever be,' Sax sighed.

'Today we'll find your 'Jesus', then tomorrow we'll call in on Moses. We'd better make sure we don't set fire to any bushes while we're there,' said Harper.

'Oh shut up,' spat Sax angrily.

Harper pressed the switches on the panel which jutted out from the wall on his side. The machine came alive with a dull high voltage electrical hum. The noise got louder and louder. Both men put their hands to their ears.

Then…nothing. Sax looked up and listened. There was nothing to hear. The loud hum had gone. So too had the soft hum that the machine always had, that he hadn't really noticed until now that it wasn't there. The everyday hustle and bustle outside the house, that he'd heard before Harper started up the sphere, was gone.

That's odd, certainly, thought Sax. Deep down, he hadn't ever really expected anything to happen, even when Harper explained how the time machine worked. He had shown him the maths, the theory, the technology that he had invented purely for this experiment. Harper had mentioned something about 'the latent energy in mercury' and some new theory of magnetic fields and neutrino tracing. What nonsense, Sax had thought. It couldn't work. It shouldn't work. But something had happened. Harper was unconscious, his spindly frame hunched unceremoniously forward in his seat. Only the seatbelt kept him from falling to the floor. Sax undid his own seatbelt, stepped over to Harper, and straightened him back into place. He still had a pulse, and he was breathing. Sax then looked at his own watch. It said five-forty, Jerusalem time. That can't be right, he thought. They activated the machine at four o'clock. Could we have been unconscious for over an hour? Possibly. Sax remembered the pain at hearing the sound. The sound must have made him pass out. He opened the hatch, thinking that he would go and fetch some water and splash it on Harper's face to wake him up. As the hatch opened, cool air rushed in, ever so slightly perfumed in some way. Sax looked out, fully expecting to see the bare walls of their rented apartment; instead, he saw nothing, just blackness. The light from the inside of the Time Sphere shone out through the small hatch, but found nothing to illuminate. Sax panicked. He felt his stomach churn.

Back in his seat, Harper groaned and slowly came to. His head felt as though it was swimming round, he felt nauseous. 'Never… like this before. It must be…must be the distance… much greater than before.' He looked up to see Sax, still standing by the open hatch, his face ashen white.

'Well?' said Harper, recovering his composure. 'Did it work?'

Sax didn't reply. He just stood there.

Harper got to his feet, stumbled to the opening and looked out. 'We're there,' he announced calmly. 'It worked.' He pushed past Sax and clambered out of the sphere. This was now a lot easier than entering the machine as it had become buried almost a metre deep in compacted dry soil. The machine stood alone, not near any buildings of any kind, looking like a strange dome. Harper went back inside and retrieved a large coarsely woven cloth and proceeded to cover the dome as best he could. 'Bring the torches will you?' whispered Harper, emerging from the darkness behind the camouflaged machine.

Sax climbed out, brandishing two medium sized torches. Harper lit them with a pocket cigarette lighter and took one from Sax. 'Let's have a look around,' he said.

'I don't think we should,' said Sax nervously. 'Not just yet. Let's wait till morning.'

'Oh, come on,' said Harper. 'Just a quick look around, and we'll come straight back. We're inside the city walls. We're quite safe.'

Even though he spoke with confidence, Harper didn't feel very safe. It had all been a game until now. He couldn't pretend to himself that he wasn't so far from the comfort of his own world, surrounded by the familiar technology that made him feel secure. He would still put on a pretence for Sax, who seemed to have lost his initial fear now, much to Harper's annoyance.

Their eyes became used to the intense darkness now and they could make out a few lights in the distance. Somewhere far away a dog barked.

'It must be very late at night. Everyone's asleep,' whispered Harper.

'Those lights could be the temple,' added Sax excitedly. 'I really must see that.' He turned back to Harper. 'Now remember. Whatever happens, whatever we see, we must not get involved with anyone or anything.'

'Yes, yes,' said Harper impatiently. 'We are observers only.'

'God knows what will happen if anyone finds out we're from the future. We'll have to make sure no-one finds the Time Sphere. Are you sure...?' Sax stopped, listening. 'I can hear footsteps. Someone's coming!'

Sure enough, walking straight towards them out of the gloom was what looked like a Roman soldier.

'Quick, put the torches out!' exclaimed Harper.

'Too late, I think he's seen us,' Sax said in dismay.

The soldier approached them slowly. He was clearly taller than both of them, dressed in battle shorts and tunic with a cloak around him. In his left hand he bore a torch. He spoke to them in Greek, a strange dialect that neither man understood. They could smell alcohol on the soldier's breath. His tone was questioning. Harper was terrified, and it was Sax who attempted to speak. A hushed, shuffling sound came from behind the soldier. He spun round to be met with three scruffily dressed men, one of whom had already plunged a dagger into the soldier's shoulder. The soldier shouted in alarm before falling to his knees. One of the other two men spotted Harper and Sax, shouted something, and ran off. The other hesitated. Harper and Sax were frozen to the spot as the dagger-wielding man retrieved his knife and dealt another blow, this time nearer the chest. He gave Harper and Sax a passing glance before he dropped the dagger at the soldier's feet then raced off with the other man into the darkness. Harper and Sax were left alone with the soldier lying spread-eagle on the floor, blood flowing thick and dark from his wounds.

Harper knelt down and examined the soldier's wounds. He was dying. He ripped off part of his cloak and attempted to staunch the bleeding. Sax picked up the evil looking dagger. He noticed a group of lights in the distance growing nearer.

'Someone else is coming now. We'd better go,' said Sax nervously.

'No,' replied Harper. 'Even in this time, this man can be saved. We've got to help him.'

'Oh come on,' Sax said under his breath. The sound of shouting and feet running was much louder now. Sax ran off, back in the direction of the Time Sphere just as half a dozen soldiers appeared behind Harper. One of them grabbed him and pulled him to his feet.

'No, don't stop me. I'm trying to save him!' Harper blurted out in English. Before he could repeat it in Hebrew, a second soldier slammed his heavy fist into Harper's stomach, knocking his breath from him and causing him to double up.

Another soldier appeared, dragging Sax, the dagger still in his hand. The soldiers spoke to one another as two of them picked up the dying man. Harper made another attempt to explain. He spoke in a broken mixture of Greek and Hebrew.

'Didn't do it. I didn't do it,' blurted out Sax, in Hebrew.

The soldiers dragged them both off.

Harper and Sax spent the rest of their first night in first century Jerusalem in what appeared to be a small dungeon. They sat silently on the straw and dust covered dirt floor for most of the time. It was Sax who spoke first.

'What do you think you were playing at? We could have got away. Why didn't you run, you idiot? We could have been safely back in the sphere now,' he said.

'I just wanted to do what I could to save him,' replied Harper angrily.

'You fool,' spat Sax. 'I told you not to interfere didn't I? 'Observers' you said. Suddenly our sight-seeing tour turns into one man's mercy mission.'

'That man could have been saved,' responded Harper.

'But he wasn't, was he?' Sax went on. 'And he wouldn't have

been if we hadn't arrived either. Those men must have been Zealots or something. They were fighting for freedom for the people of Israel. They were attacking the Romans all the time. You wanted to save one man?'

'Oh shut up, Sax,' said Harper. 'You always did want to look after number one.'

'You seemed to have changed your tune suddenly. One minute you're planning to murder Hitler; then you're saving someone's life.'

'There is a bit of a difference there.' Harper's anger was building, but controllable at the moment.

'Oh really?' said Sax. 'Well look where your morality has got us,' sneered Sax.

'I don't see you coming up with any quick solutions to this predicament,' Harper responded sharply.

'And what do you suggest? I suppose you had this all worked into your oh-so-clever plan?'

'Not quite,' Harper said calmly. 'We'll simply explain what happened. We don't even look Jewish. We could hardly be Zealots. What possible motive would we have for trying to kill a Roman sentry in the middle of the city?'

'I must say I don't feel that my future is safe in your hands. The Romans are not going to be easily convinced by you. In fact, you've never convinced anyone to do anything,' said Sax.

'Except you, of course,' replied Harper.

'I didn't believe that you could actually do it. To build a time machine, my God,' Sax replied sarcastically.

'You should have believed me.'

'Oh shut up!' shouted Sax.

His shout brought the guard's attention. It must have been morning outside, but inside the cell, it was still very dark. The men could only see the guards through a small gap that ran along the wall at eye level. Both Harper and Sax dashed over to it and, independent of each other, attempted to proclaim their innocence.

'I didn't do it, believe me...' blurted out Sax, in Hebrew.

'Look, there were some men. They attacked the soldier...' said Harper, also in Hebrew.

'We know what happened,' said one of the guards.

'Good,' said Harper. 'Then you'll know that I was trying to save him'.

The soldiers laughed, perhaps at Harper's words, or more likely at his accent. They looked at Sax. 'You had the knife in your hand,' said one to Sax.

'No, no, I just picked it up,' Sax said in panic.

'And you were making sure the Centurion was dead,' the other guard said to Harper.

'Oh no, you're wrong. I was trying to stop the bleeding.'

'You rebel scum,' said the first guard to them both. 'You fight with the honor-less tactics of thieves and murderers, all the time proclaiming your great cause, and when you are caught, you babble and bray like cowardly mules.' He spat on them. 'I'm only too pleased that the Procurator is here. There'll be no uprising today. You'll be paraded out as an example to your rebel friends no doubt.'

They both laughed again and moved out of sight from the gap in the cell wall.

'So much for you talking us out of here,' said Sax after they realised the gravity of the situation.

'I didn't hear you backing up my story,' said Harper. 'If you hadn't concentrated on saving you own neck, we could have convinced them enough that there is a shadow of doubt over what they think happened.'

'I had the knife, remember,' said Sax. 'How was I supposed to talk my way out of that one?'

'You picked it up,' retorted Harper. 'You were probably looking to see if it would look good in your collection of Roman artifacts.'

That was enough for Sax. He struck Harper with a blow to the head. Harper, although already weakened from the previous punch he had received, managed to swipe back at Sax, hitting him on his nose, causing it to bleed. Both men slumped to the floor again, in silence.

A little over an hour later, they were dragged out, still protesting their innocence, and brought into an open courtyard. The bright sunlight made their eyes hurt. There were a few soldiers walking across the yard. They paid no attention to the two bedraggled strangers. In the centre of the circular yard was a tall pillar with ropes attached. Nearby was an assortment of whips. Another Roman walked up to them, flanked by two centurions. He was dressed slightly differently to the two that had ushered them outside.

Sax addressed him. 'You must be the Procurator, Sir. I have been arrested under false pretences,' he said.

The Roman didn't look at Sax, but spoke to one of the guards.

'Who is this fool who thinks I could be Pilate?'

'A Zealot sir,' replied the guard.

Harper and Sax protested again.

The guard continued, 'We found them near the body of a murdered centurion last night. This one was bent over him,' he said indicating Harper, 'and the other held a bloodied dagger.'

'There seems to have been some mistake,' said Harper.

'Oh?' said the Roman, looking at the two prisoners for the first time.

'We are not Zealots. We are not even Jewish. Two men attacked your Centurion. I was trying to stop the bleeding when your men arrived.'

'That has the ring of truth,' said the Roman. 'You do indeed look unlike any Jew I have seen. But this man was found with the knife. You don't deny that?'

'No, but…'

Before Harper could finish, Sax blurted out, 'I just picked the knife up. The attacker had dropped it.'

'Oh, and what attacker would have time to withdraw his blade? And why drop it at your feet? It seems to me to be a curious story, and quite ridiculous.'

'There was no-one else nearby, sir,' added one of the guards.

'Right,' said the Roman. 'Which leaves only you two.'

Sax said pointed at Harper and for seemingly no reason said, 'He killed him.'

'What?' said Harper in disbelief.

'I tried to stop him,' Sax went on, 'got the dagger away from him, but it was too late. That's when your men arrived.'

The Roman sighed and addressed the guards. 'I think I have had quite enough of this nonsense. Take these criminals away and flog them. At least then we'll have some bounty to recount to the Procurator when he arrives.'

Harper and Sax were dragged off, kicking and screaming at the guards and each other. The Roman turned to his aides.

'Pilate will make his speech to the Jews at the Temple today. They are all going to gather there for one of their ethnic festivals or something. Tradition has it that, on this day certain prisoners should be released. I'll speak to Pilate and suggest that he honors that tradition. He can hand over one of those two fools. It might just keep the rabble tame.'

'But sir,' protested one of the centurions. 'Those men are

murderers. We already have two other prisoners.'

It was another hour or so later after their flogging that Harper and Sax were dragged out from their cell for the last time.

'What will happen to us now?' asked Sax exhaustedly.

'The Procurator is making is speech,' said a guard. 'You'll know soon enough.'

They were taken down a corridor back to the courtyard where they had been flogged earlier. A centurion walked over to their guards.

'What news?' said the guard.

'It was ridiculous,' he replied. 'The rabble cheered for that man that killed two of our men last week.'

'What's going on?' asked Harper.

The soldiers didn't answer. Two large beams of wood were brought over to them.

'Lie down,' a soldier said coldly. Both men could only do as they were told. They were now too weak to protest their innocence. The soldiers tied their arms to the beams and they were instructed to get back up on their feet.

'Now walk,' said the soldier.

They were marched out of the Roman barracks and onto the streets of the city. Sax looked around and noticed how ordinary it looked, and how little Jerusalem had changed over the millennia. Harper just felt sick. The red wheals on his bare back stung. He had also developed a black eye from Sax's earlier punch. The men marched on through crowds of people, past the Temple. Sax didn't have the energy to look up at it. Most of the people looked away. Soon the crowds thinned out, and they passed through the city walls and walked on grass, past a number of squat trees until they stopped at the foot of a hill. They were then pulled in another direction, round to the back of the hill and were made to climb the much shallower slope.

After reaching the top, they both felt like collapsing, but the soldiers and temple guards who met them at the flat summit held them steady. They stood next to a huge wooden scaffolding with various rope attachments. Ropes were attached to the beams on their shoulders, and the men were moved to the front of the scaffolding, in front of small group of people, who were all facing the other way.

Harper and Sax hardly had time to think before they were hoisted up onto the scaffolding. Harper felt his ribs and stomach drop away from him as his feet left the ground. He felt his arms come under enormous pressure as they tried to hold up his body weight on their own. He found it very hard to breathe, and a sharp pain developed in his chest. He looked to his right to see the heavier Sax, and thought how he would be worse off. Their feet were about three metres from the ground when they felt the hoisting cease. The horizontal beams were then hammered into place.

Looking down they could see a procession leaving the city gates from where they had come. The trail moved nearer until it was out of sight, obviously following the same trail which would lead them round the back of the hill. Harper closed his eyes and tried to ignore the pain. The pain! He had forgotten the time experiment now. He had forgotten Sax and the encounter with the Romans. He had forgotten everything, even who he was. He didn't look up again until a chorus of wailing stirred him from his painful delirium.

The crowd in front of the scaffolding was much larger now. All eyes were on him—no wait—they were looking just to the right of him. Harper slowly moved his head to the right. That simple movement upset the angle of his body and sent rivers of pain shooting through his nervous system. Just beyond the extent of his own right hand, he could see a man whose wrists had been nailed onto the horizontal beam, not tied with a rope as his were. He was thankful for that. As he looked at the bloody nail sticking out from the man's hand, the man's head turned. The face was one of pain. Rivulets of blood trickled down from a circular barbed construction on his head like a cap of thorns, and had matted his long hair. The man's eyes met Harper. They burned deep into Harper's. The face was familiar, but Harper couldn't remember who it reminded him of. Harper wanted to look away, but couldn't take his eyes off that gaze. Oddly he felt his pain subside a little, but was filled with sadness. This man shouldn't be here, he thought. This is a good man. Something's wrong. At that point, his delirium suddenly left him. He felt a strength well up within him, collecting in his tear ducts. He knew who this man was! It seemed so obvious now. He felt the strength to speak.

Sax looked across at Harper. He shouted over, 'You bastard, Harper. You bastard. You've killed us. You and your stupid pride.'

Harper breathed in, trying to gain the strength to respond. 'We deserve to be here after what we've done and what we've thought. I thought I could escape time, that I was somehow separate from it, only to become trapped in it, to become part of history just like everybody else.' Harper remembered how he had thought he was amongst the greatest geniuses who had ever lived. That had all changed now. He had been caught out. He now felt like a small cog in a very large machine. He had found his place in history all right, two-thousand years before he was due to be born. He looked over at Sax again. 'Look at this man. Don't you realise who this is? What has he done to be strung up here with us?' he panted. Sax wasn't listening. Harper turned his head to the man nailed next to him, who had turned his head towards the ground.

'Yeshua' said Harper.

The man turned to face him again.

'Thank you,' Harper said with all his might. 'You have given me something I never knew I could have, only to find I seemed to have had it all the time. Please...' he paused, gasping for air, 'Please remember me when you come into your kingdom.' His head slumped down on his chest, panting.

The man spoke. His voice was calm and clear, even though he must have been in great pain.

'Believe me. Today, you and I will be in paradise.'

Harper smiled. He didn't feel the pain anymore. He didn't feel anything anymore. He closed his eyes.

Epilogue:
Why our children need to read and write Science Fiction

The starting point didn't ever bother me. The teacher may have told us to write a story about our families, the supermarket, the past, a walk in the woods or to finish a story from his opening paragraph or anything…

Whatever it was, I'd write just two paragraphs before incorporating a brightly lit saucer landing in the woods, a visitor from the future, a portal into the past, people revealed as aliens, or robots, a curse from ancient Egypt, a primordial evil hiding in a dark lake, a creature in a zoo that turns out to be sentient, an alien invasion is really an intergalactic game of tiddlywinks…

Me aged 13: "He strained his eyes to fix on a unusual shape which was slowly lowering. It was a large saucer shaped object with a gleaming metal hull, reflecting the snow and trees."

Teachers response: "You are a cunning devil! You managed to introduce what is obviously an interest of yours into." (sic)

I always turned the premise into Science Fiction.

And I was criticised and marked down for doing so.

I was driven by a 'search for interesting' (to me, a definition of creativity) and a desire to twist the mundane by a turn of the screw to see the ordinary afresh, from a different perspective, to explore the unexpected and to find rationale in the unexplained.

But my teachers didn't agree. They felt it was childish and unsophisticated.

I think this is a shame. More than a shame. A crisis.

To an outsider, Science Fiction as a genre is still misunderstood and the tendency with poor writing (in some books, some television and films) to rely on clichéd concepts such as unimaginative spaceships, mad robots and generic aliens makes many people overlook the main purpose of Science Fiction (also referred to as SF by purists, but never Sci-Fi). This bias and misunderstanding has in the past alienated many, especially young girls from the genre. It's interesting to note that the new production of *Doctor Who* set out with re-dressing this balance and have achieved it with the ratio of girls and boys watching the programme almost equal.

Science Fiction has the unique capabilities to allow a child to explore themselves and their world in non-literal ways.

Science Fiction's alternative title is 'Speculative Fiction'.

It is stories that are driven by a 'what if?' question. The answer to this question is answered by the story using real-world science to extrapolate it and to drive the characters and the plot. Science Fiction keeps most things constant and has one or a few variables that can then be explored.

This is the essential difference between Science Fiction and Fantasy, although the lines are often blurred.

Star Trek, the television and film series is Science Fiction. It has a number of plot devices that are beyond our current technology including teleportation and faster-than-light travel. But within the story framework these technologies are explained in scientific, believable ways with their own rules and limitations that are kept constant within the story. In fact, those two technologies are plot device conceits and not the driving force for the story. They are story enablers. In reality it would take centuries to travel to the stars, the distance between them is so great and it is a complicated and long-winded process to safely travel from orbit to land on a planet. The 'Warp Drive' and 'Transporter' fictional technologies remove the mundane to tell a much more interesting story. The story of *Star Trek*, the speculative 'what if?' is: 'what would it be like to travel to strange new worlds and visit new civilisations?'

Harry Potter is not Science Fiction. It too has unrealistic devices, and they are consistent within the world of the story, but these are not explained in any other way other than 'magic' and cannot be extrapolated from our understanding of real-world technology. This makes *Harry Potter* Fantasy.

When it comes to examining the film series *Star Wars* as a genre, people tend to make an interesting mistake. They often think it is 'futuristic' because it features robots and spaceships and yet the opening phrase that begins the film is 'a long time ago, in a galaxy far, far away'. This is the same as the well-known start to many a story, 'once upon a time' and frames *Star Wars*, like *Cinderella*, as a fairy tale and not overall, Science Fiction. No serious attempt is made in *Star Wars* to rationalise space travel, how light sabres work, how the robots appear to be conscious and what The Force really is. *Star Wars* is fantasy disguised as Science Fiction. It's interesting that it's other writers of the expanded universe and fan fiction that have taken it upon themselves to turn the *Star Wars* universe into a Science Fiction one.

Doctor Who is yet more complicated. The premise is Science Fiction: 'an alien who looks like a man, travels through time and space in a time machine made by a lost civilisation that resembles a 1960s Police Box that is bigger on the inside.' But unlike other franchises, *Doctor Who* changes genre from story to story, some stories are straight Science Fiction, some are fantasy, some thriller or historical drama, comedy, tragedy and even romance. Doctor Who is better described as 'Science Fantasy'.

When teaching children storytelling, I believe it is important for them to realise which overall genre their story is fitting into if it is to include what appear to be Science Fiction elements: are they creating a whole new world with its own rules and physical laws where literally anything can happen? Is so, that's fantasy (the most solid example in Literature may well be Tolkien's *The Lord of the Rings*). Or are they keeping most of the rules of the known world and for dramatic effect or as a speculative story driver, choosing to twist, re-invent or magnify one or more real-world rules. If so, they are writing Science Fiction.

This is why Science Fiction is so enthralling, so exciting to read and to write, and so useful to us as a civilisation. It allows us to look at an aspect of ourselves from a different perspective. The stories explored in *Star Trek* are not really about space travel, aliens and the future, they are all about fragments of ourselves, now. In one story, Captain Kirk and his crew are bemused by a race of people who have one side of their faces black and the other white and yet are fighting each other. When asked why, a man retorts, "Isn't it obvious! He has the white side on the left and black on the right and we have it the other way round!". (*Let That Be Your Last Battlefield*). This Science Fiction allows the story to explore the ridiculous nature of racism.

Children's relationship to Science Fiction is usually based on the magical attraction of the fantastical otherness of outer space, aliens and the excitement of adventure. But it can also be the appeal of a relationship with a creature such as a robot or alien with whom the child can connect in their own way on their own terms without the trappings of their own weaknesses.

This is why *Star Wars* worked in the first place: children identified with the cute robots in a way that adults couldn't and would not. This is why children, especially boys, still love steam engines, cars and other machines which they can easily bestow consciousness into. It also connects to the most primordial of children's secret fantasies: the imaginary friend.

The mobile dustbin-like robot, R2D2, in *Star Wars* is really a modern variation of the teddy bear.

Soon after we had seen the film, a colleague of my Dad's was round at our house. He'd been to see the original film, as had nearly everyone, to 'see what all the fuss was about'. The opening scene, as you may remember, features no human characters. For the first ten minutes, we are expected to engage with a gold metal man and a walking, twerping dustbin on wheels in the white corridors of a spaceship that has been swallowed by a giant spaceship. Baddies appear in the form of white plastic-clad soldiers, their faces hidden by helmets, led by a black cloaked pantomime villain compete with black skull-like mask. No wonder Frank walked out after ten minutes after seeing this rubbish.

But that's not what we children saw. As a six-and-a-half

year old, I saw the fear and trepidation of the gold robot. I saw the determination of the small domed headed clever robot. I saw that they were the characters we were engaging with and that they were carrying the story and that the humans and stormtroopers fighting in the background were incidental to their story, the goodies, our friends. After ten minutes we knew that C3PO had reluctantly agreed to take part in an important mission he didn't understand. We knew that R2D2 carried secrets that must be kept from the baddies. Children have the ability to see a story, to see the elements of characterisation, emotion and motivation in what to the adults were inanimate objects. In short, children's imaginations are less literal, more hungry for meaning, more powerful. Adults want it all on plate, often too bored and in need of instant gratification and explanation to actually fire up their long unused imagination.

So many modern stories, designed for children, fail to engage in the way something like *Star Wars* can, like all fairy tales can, because they lack the depth of meaning that the child can find for themselves and use the story, as it was intended, as a tool to find answers to their own problems.

I was born at exactly the right time to live through the *Star Wars* phenomenon as it happened. I wouldn't have it any other way. To older, more boring unimaginative people, *Star Wars* was just a film, albeit a very popular one with people queuing around the block to get tickets to see it, that broke new ground with special effects. But to me it was like witnessing the Gospel.

I was the last to see it at my school. I was six years old. I badgered Sean as to what it was like. I knew there were robots in it, a gold humanoid one and a small Dalek-like one. I asked him if R2D2 had a gun, did he shoot like Daleks did? Sean couldn't remember. Couldn't remember? How could he not remember? I was busting to see it. I started to guess what it was about and made up a story that I thought might fit the bill.

We went to Newcastle one Saturday. There was an enormous poster of Darth Vader's head covering the front of the cinema. I'd only been to the cinema once before, to see a Children's Film Foundation film about a hot air balloon. We were given a programme in the foyer that introduced us to the concepts in the film.

The next day we had *Star Wars* Weetabix for breakfast. There were transfers in the packet that you could rub onto a diorama on the back of the box, of Darth Vader and Ben Kenobi's lightsabre duel on the Death Star. We had to finish the packet before we could cut the box up. We'd never eaten so much Weetabix.

To my generation of children, the story of *Star Wars*, which was a re-telling of ancient fairy stories, was so potent in its splendor as an exciting alien tale, that it entered our consciousness. It provided what all fairy stories provide: a moral template for good and evil, the concept of the hero's journey, the quest, where obstacles must be overcome and sacrifices made. The characters are archetypal, but still colourful. Some adults at the time found it hard to see the depth in it and even with the mania that surrounded its original release where people queued around the block to get into cinemas. They would not have predicted its longevity. Even its creator George Lucas didn't know the secret of the success of the original film (and the two subsequent films that formed the original trilogy). The prequels that followed twenty years later lacked something. Even though they were more spectacular and exotic that the originals there was perhaps a lack of depth or mystery and less room for the imagination to weave within the story. This isn't surprising or unusual. It's not the artist's job to understand their art. That's the job the audience.

That was 1977, Jubilee year. Last year it was Jubilee year again and 35 years later to the day, I opened up the Sacred Glass Cabinet at the top of the stairs. It contains my 200+ *Star Wars* Action Figures. Mabel (4), Verity (nearly 2) and I selected a (large) collection and we took them downstairs, and along with lego we created an adventure story. (Neither of the girls have yet seen *Star Wars*). This is what they came up with:

Princess Leia (in Bespin outfit), R2D2, C3PO, TC14, and

a friendly Jawa arrived in their snowspeeder to an ancient ruined pyramid which the team suspected contained a great secret. R2 went in through the gap in the wall, but didn't return. C3PO was too nervous to investigate so Princess Leia called for help and Chewbacca and Hammerhead arrived in a landspeeder. Hammerhead's big hands managed to move more bricks and Chewie went inside only to be met by a fierce Gammorean Guard. It turned out he wasn't a baddie, he wanted to warn them of the unsafe structure. Chewie and Bossk went carefully in and pulled out R2 and a Death Star Droid who was in need of repair. 9D9 and Powerdroid got him working again and he told of the treasure that was still inside the pyramid. Working together they removed enough bricks to pull the treasure out. The Princess changed into her ceremonial white dress and it was time for everyone's lunch. Stories happen!

My girls were doing exactly what I'd done all those years ago. *Star Wars* figures are wonderful because they are so interesting. Palitoy seemed to deliberately make figures of all the minor characters and leave out many of the main ones. You couldn't get Grand Moff Tarkin (played on screen by Peter Cushing) who's central to the story. But you could get Death Star Commander, who you see for two seconds in the background.

My brother and I never played with them to re-create scenes from the film. Instead we'd create characteristics and adventures for these lesser-known creatures, people and droids. R5D4, Dengar or Snaggletooth may only have appeared in the films for less than a second, but that's what made them so fascinating. They could be whoever we wanted them to be.

I never got a Millennium Falcon playset, or the so obviously not-to-scale rubbish cardboard Death Star. I didn't get the Jawa Sandcrawler, Boba Fett's Slave One spaceship or the exciting giant AT-AT snow walkers either. They were all far too expensive and elaborate.

But I've never been so grateful for anything from my childhood as I am for NOT getting those toys for Christmas because it meant that instead I made my own.

I collected my Mum's perfume bottle tops, cardboard, any plastic packaging. It was all saved up, glued together and painted. I had far better playsets than the ones prescribed by Palitoy and learnt model making into the bargain.

Oh, and the story I expected to see before I saw the actual film? I wrote it down and developed it as my own secret movie franchise with its own characters, robots and monsters. I even made action figures of them using Fimo thermo setting plastic. (There's a short section of one of my comic strips of those stories at the front of this book).

When children desire to use Science Fiction techniques and motifs, they may already be using their writing to explore themselves and their world, without any need for guidance and literal knowledge.

On the surface they may conjure up spaceships and monsters, but don't let these fool us. They may already be using these devices in the same way as the greatest Science Fiction authors, H.G Wells, Issac Asimov, Arthur C. Clarke, John Wyndham or Ray Bradbury, did, as cloaked methods of exploring and explaining their own inner worlds in a way that straightforward 'literal' fiction cannot.

I don't think I'm particularly unique in having an imagination.   Every child has one. But it needs to be developed and encouraged. I think it was mainly good luck that I became embroiled in Science Fiction and fantasy at the age I did in the way I did. *Star Wars* was such a good vehicle for the imagination. It still is. It's a simple story, but so well told with such background depth that's perfect fertile ground for the seeds of a child's imagination to take root, explore and grow.

Boring, literal, obvious stories are at risk of quenching the fire of a child's imagination. If they haven't found the tools to engage with objects and people to begin creating their own stories early enough, they may switch off their creativity and become uninterested vessels for easy stories, flashes, bangs and the oh-so-quick editing of fast-food dull television, just like so many tedious adults.

This is why stories for children should not be too safe,

too sanitised or too obvious. We, as parents and teachers must try not to explain the meaning of such tales but encourage the child to search for and find their own meaning, which may change with subsequent readings and at different points in their lives. This is the creative process of the transition from reader to writer, from consumer to creator.

Our job is to help facilitate these new creators. By reading a good story, a child's mind becomes co-creator with the original author. This is the first stage to a fulfilling, meaningful, self-directed life of significance.

I believe we need to teach children how to play and invent, to experiment, to try things out and take risks – not all of them can learn how to do it on their own. And I believe we need to give them the tools of play but need to be careful not to over prescribe too tight a formula and format so that anything and everything is still possible. With many modern toys and especially computer games I feel there's a real risk of dumbing down. Anything and everything is still possible, and Science Fiction provides the rules on how to make anything happen.

If your child finds more interest in the box the toy came in rather than the toy itself – keep watch, something interesting may be happening in that imagination of theirs...

You can read about my own creative writing project for schools here: **www.sunmakers.co.uk**

About the author

Ayd Instone is head of Physics at Fyling Hall School. He runs a creative writing club *The Intergalactic Writers' Guild* to encourage students (aged 11 to 18) to write their own stories. This helps with both their English and Science studies. Ayd has a Masters in Teaching and Learning from the University of Oxford. Prior to teaching he was an international speaker on creativity and innovation, a singer/songwriter, graphic artist and an occasional comedian. He lives in Robin Hood's Bay with his wife, three children and two cats.

Sometimes he writes on his blog: http://aydinstone.wordpress.com/

You can see videos of Ayd performing on YouTube and at:

www.aydinstone.com

@aydinstone

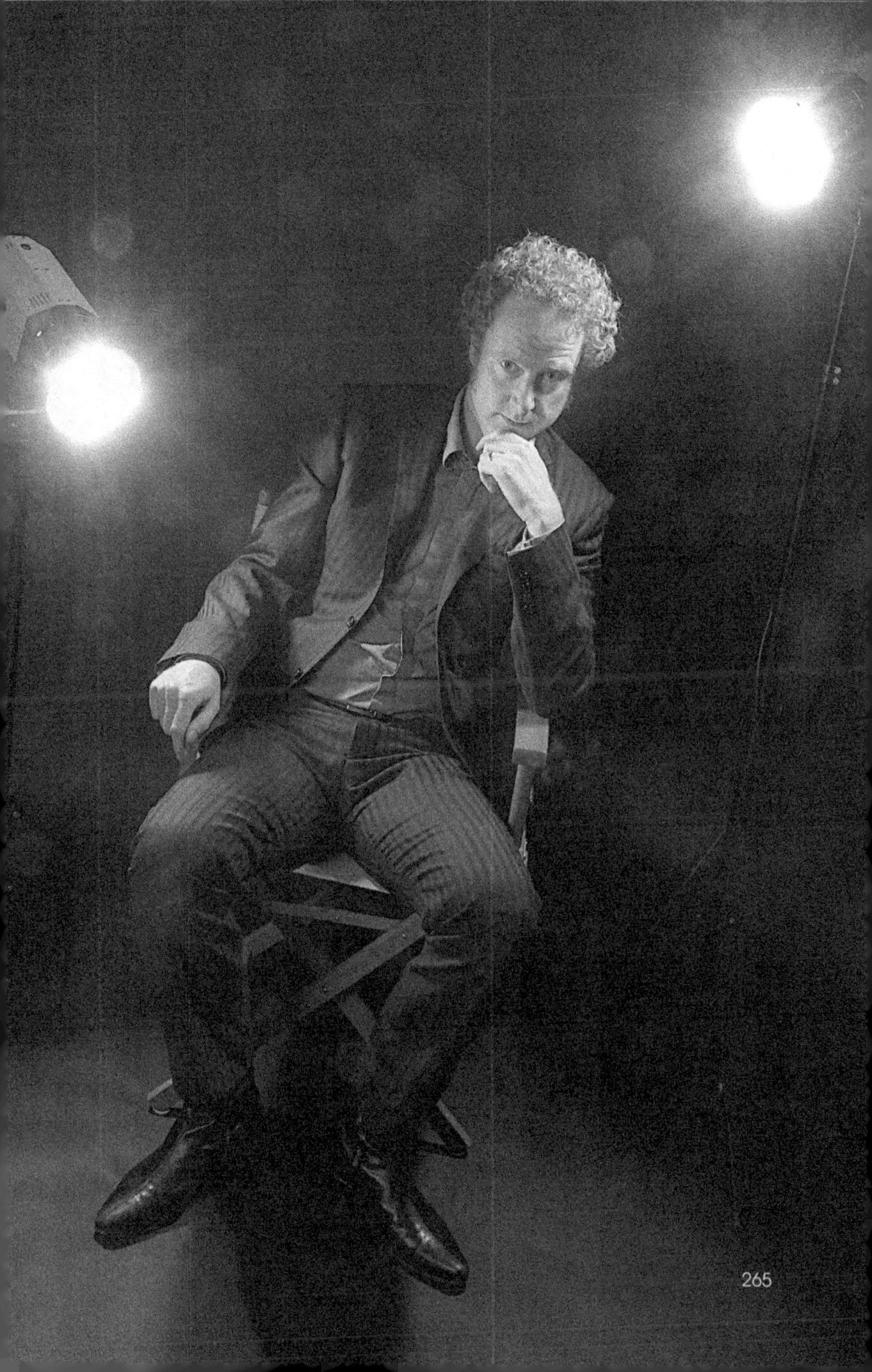

www.ingramcontent.com/pod-product-compliance
Lightning Source LLC
Chambersburg PA
CBHW071455170626
46811CB00007B/2589